THE KILLING GAME

SAGE MITCHELL

TIME TO DIE

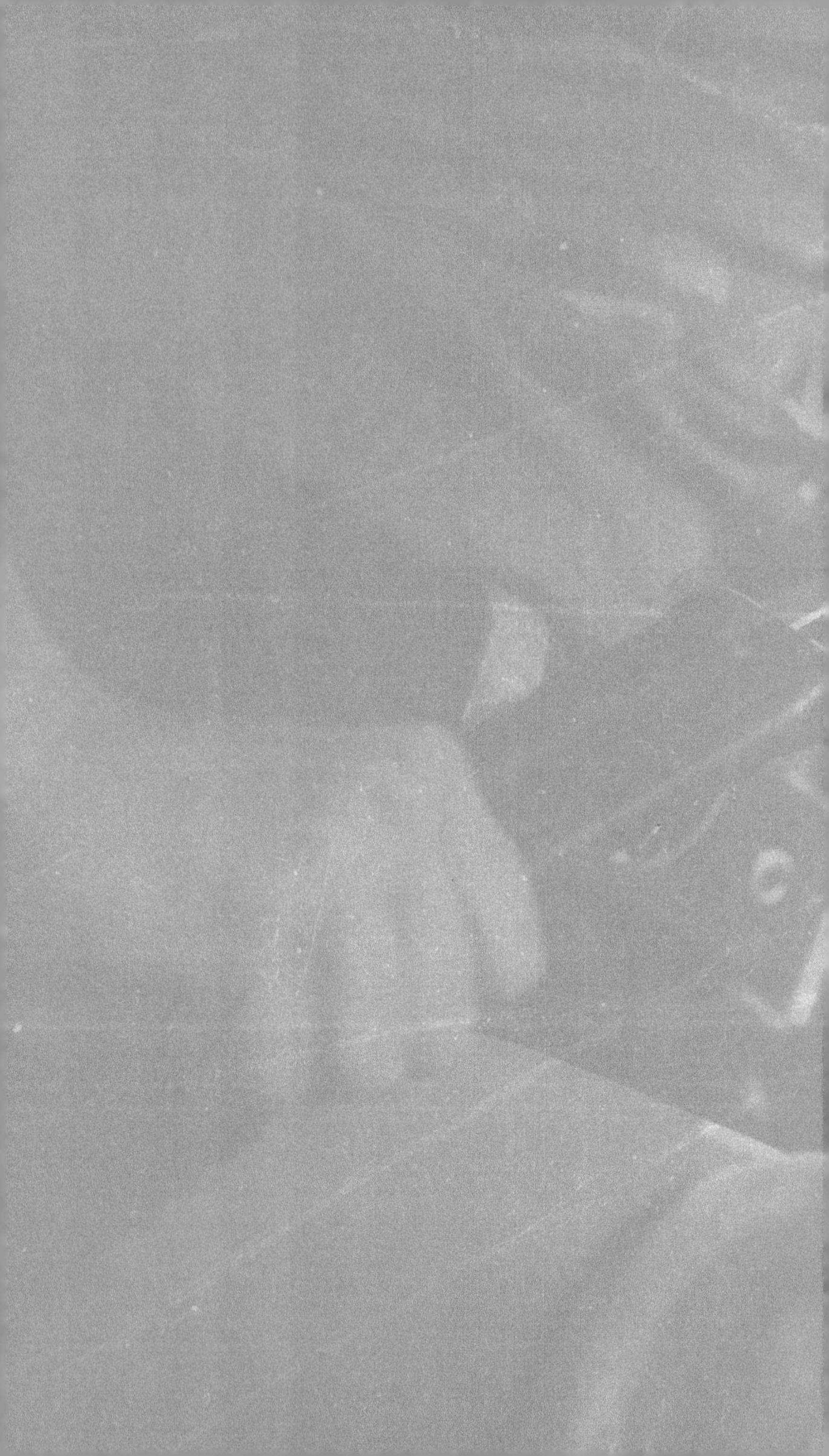

FORWARD

A friendly reminder to everyone who reads dark, spicy books. This isn't a happy go-lucky story. The "spice" in question is borderline dubcon or noncon. There is no traditional HEA. This is horror erotica. It's dark, disturbing, and questionable.

Let's clarify.

In real life? Consent is KEY.

In these books? Anything and everything goes.

So, even though this story isn't nearly as dark as it could be. Even If you think the content warning list is "just another list"— always check in with yourself. Be honest if something is too much for you. Take breaks. Put the book down and come back later. I promise the story will still be there when you return. Your mental health matters. <3

Trigger Warnings:
* Murder
* Cursing
* Kidnapping
* Open Door Scenes
* Knife Play
* Blood Play
* Asphyxiation
* Sexual Assault
* DubCon/NonCon
* Corpse Mutilation
* Degradation
* Necrophilia (mentioned, not on page)
* Anxiety Ticks and Attack

TIME TO DIE

The Senior Slayer is eagerly awaiting your dedication.

Now be a good little bat and turn the page.

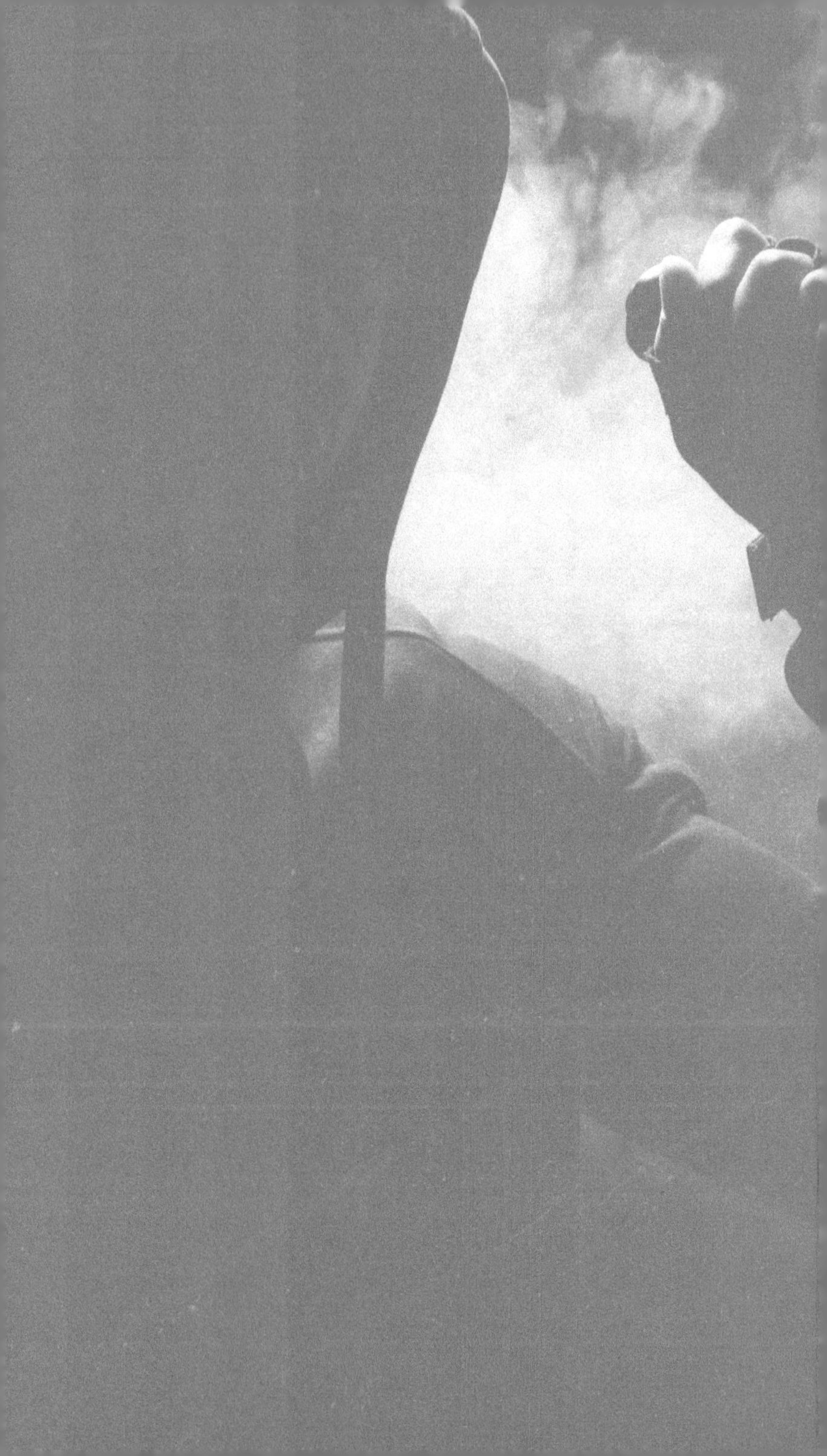

PLAYLIST

A moody little collection to get you in the killing mood. Listen in any order. Get your headphones, music player, and knife ready. It's time to die...

1. Halloweenie IV: Innards (Ashnikko)
2. MONSTER (Chandler Leighton)
3. I Can't Decide (Scissor Sisters)
4. Tamagotchi (TIMMS)
5. Witch Hunt (Chandler Leighton, DEZI)
6. Choke (Royal & the Serpent)
7. AMERICAN HORROR SHOW (SNOW WIFE)
8. FU In My Head (Cloudy June)
9. god sent me as karma (emlyn)
10. Dead To Me (Chloe Adams)
11. Mental Funeral (EHLE)
12. MURDER MY FEELINGS (Lala Sadii)
13. Lights Out (bludnymph)

TIME TO DIE

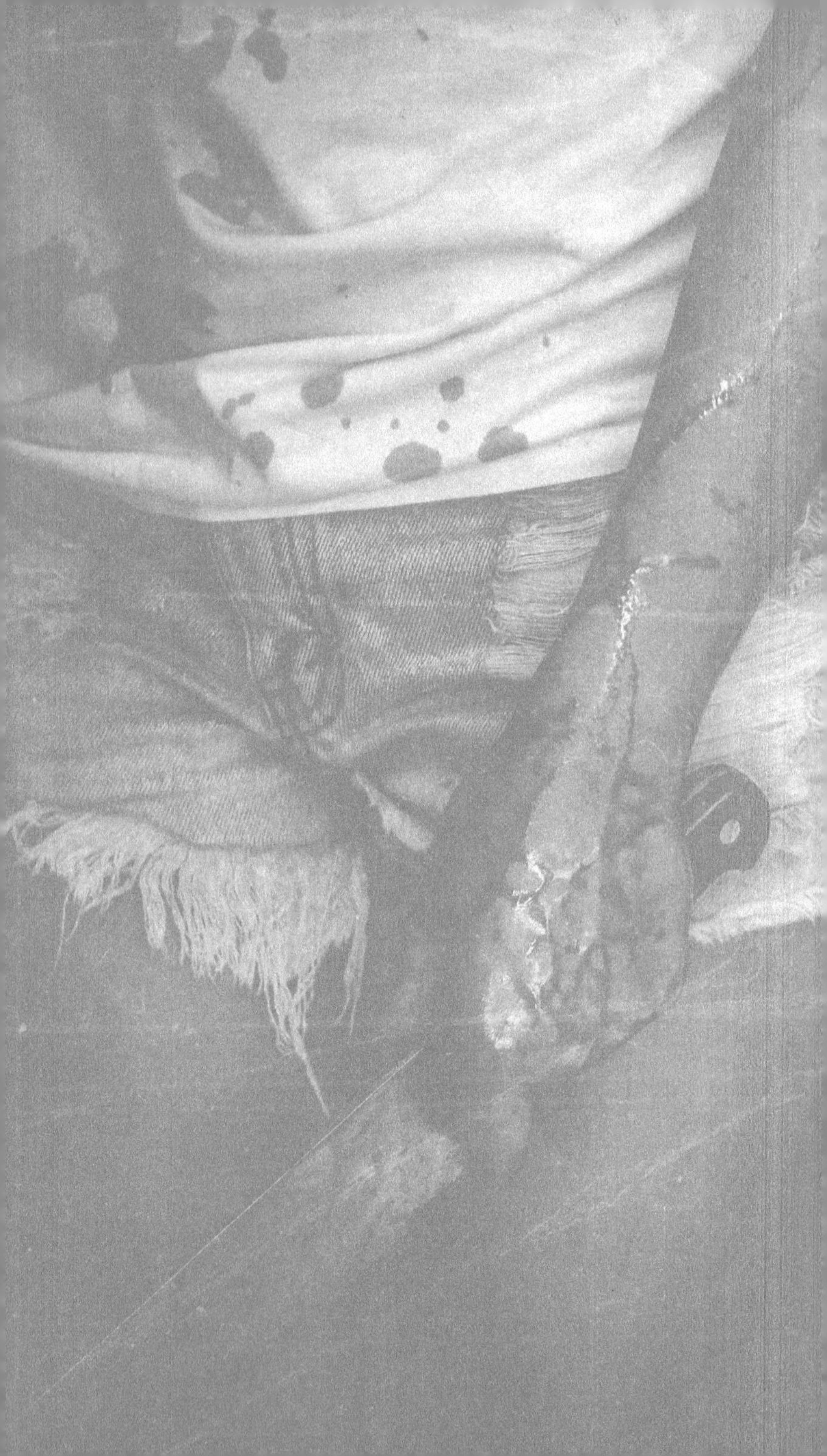

PROLOGUE

ASHE

"You're fucking disgusting. I bet your micro peen is so hard for this right now."

The words leave my mouth before I have time to think of the consequences.

I watch as the killer stalks closer to me, watching me through their skull mask. Black, haunted eyes stare back at me. The ax they used to mutilate my right leg scrapes behind them, sparking across the concrete floor of the lake shed.

Shit.

Of course, my smart ass would have some sarcastic quip before I die. The killer isn't even phased by my remark. It'd be kind of a turn on to be chased by a masked man if I wasn't about to die.

I painstakingly crawl my way to the back door with my leg dragging behind me. Fleshy, red muscle protrudes from my calf while blood gushes from the weeping orifice. The tendrils of muscle ripped from the gash trailing behind me is like a fishing line in the water. My body taunts the killer to take hold and yank me back to my death. Each breath is ragged and calculated.

Fuck. Fuck. FUCK.

Adrenaline is pumping through my veins. Everything around me is drowned out by the pounding in my ears. There's only ten feet between freedom and the most horrific death I could ever imagine. Who would've thought *this* would be how I would go out? My friends would be surprised I haven't stopped the killer yet. All those years obsessing over true crime and horror movies, for what?

Each inch feels like miles through shards of glass. The excruciating pain radiates from my mangled limb racking my body with shivers. It makes it nearly impossible to move forward. I'm going to go into shock before I make it out of here.

"Please. It doesn't have to be this way. I'm sorry," I choke out. "Gods, help me." The words don't hold the sincerity I want them to. Rage lingers in my voice. It doesn't even waiver. My words ring too strong in their conviction. I'm staring down my hunter with hatred and primal fear.

Maybe I could convince them to have mercy. It only takes a split second in a lapse of judgment to make a move. I could escape and get help.

Then I can hunt this motherfucker down and hang them with their own intestines while they watch me feed their severed cock to the local wild life.

TIME TO DIE

ONE

No one would have ever guessed I killed someone my senior year. Blurs of green and brown pass by my passenger window as I replay the scenes of my personal horror story. Red, sticky hand prints forever painted on my soul highlighting the darkest part of me. The depravity of being stalked by the worst serial killer in our town's history. Surviving, knowing what he does, but not being able to tell the tale. Instead, I write my own fucked up stories for a living. A twisted way to calm the monster lurking deep inside.

"Ashe, did you hear me?" Colton eyes me in the rear view mirror, waiting for an answer. His blue eyes are untrusting with my looming shenanigans this weekend. I chew on the string to my black *Halloween* hoodie as I stare back at the passing trees out the window. I contemplate answering him with an actual answer, but that wouldn't be any fun.

"Yes, Daddy. I heard you the first two times. No one wanders off alone or you end up in another Graveslake horror movie. I got it," I say as I meet his gaze in the rear view mirror.

It's a challenge.

He could argue with me, getting even more irritated, or he can leave it alone. It's up to him. He's always had a little hot hotheadedness in him simmering under the surface.

Colton is the stereotypical All-American boy; six foot three, built like a brick shit house, and tanned to perfection. The average girl would fawn over him like a dog in heat. I, on the other hand, find him romantically repulsive because he lacks depth. Don't get me wrong, I love him. He's the biggest goober on the planet; total golden retriever energy with a hint of pit bull. However, his reserved demeanor would never mesh with my darkness. Instead, our friendship has grown tenfold since high school. He's someone I could confine in when I needed a shoulder to lean on. With that friendship also came the pranks and bantering. I learned early on in high school how to press his buttons. Everyone in the group did. Everyone except Sam. We do it out of love, obviously.

Sam is the only one who reminds us we should be kind to each other. She doesn't believe in insults and sarcasm as a love language. It's boring, in my humble opinion, but I never faulted her for it. Everything is light and love with her. The resident hippie. I envy her way of looking at everything with rose-colored glasses.

I know better than to expect the best out of people. I learned from an early age that the people you should trust the most can turn out to be total monsters when the mask comes off. Behind closed doors, even the most pious man is filled with impulses that would make Ted Buddy or Ed Kemper blush. It only takes one little crack to let the demons out. Luckily, no one in my friend group knows the deal I made with the devil years ago. I play along as the quirky, alternative girl who's too into true crime and horrmance (Yes, that's horror with romance. I like my men morally gray and sadistic. Sue me). It's easier than explaining my sins.

"I can be your Daddy, Ashe. All you have to do is be a good girl," Jason pipes up from the front passenger seat. He turns around to face me, the smirk on his face matching the lust in his dark, amber eyes.

"That's not how the phrase goes, Jason." I roll my stony, gray eyes at him while giving him the middle finger. He laughs at me and wiggles his eyebrows, not backing down.

That's the typical response from Jason. He looks like a clone of that alternative, shy boy you had a crush on in high school. The one with the raven-dark hair coiffed to perfection, while his clothes made him look like a metal band reject. After we graduated high school, that look was complete with a full sleeve of tattoos and stretched ears to match. Just imagine any alternative TikToker you've seen recently trying to thirst trap you by quoting your favorite dark romance book. That's Jason. All that moody exterior is met with the most cocky ego possible. I can only roll my eyes so many times in a day before I get dizzy from his persistent come-ons. It's like he thinks if he chases me long enough I'll regain interest. He blew that chance a while ago. Not going to happen, my dude.

"You realize that old ghost story we heard growing up isn't real, right? I rather not bring that kind of negativity into the universe for our last trip together." Sam gives a pointed look to Colton while she curls up in her thrifted afghan. Curly, brunette hair tied up in a silk scarf flies wildly in the wind from my open window. Her green eyes are red and glazed over, likely from the joint she hit at our last rest stop. Despite all her attempts to be a ray of sunshine, she will always be my Sam who gets anxious in new situations. It doesn't matter if she's with friends or not; that social anxiety runs deep. The weed helps her mellow out. Even the most innocent of us have demons hiding inside.

Sam and I learned early on in our friendship that we compliment each other. My extroverted bluntness matches her introverted positivity. We literally became friends because I told her shitty ex-boyfriend to treat her right or I would do it for him. He didn't like that very much. Though, it did get Sam's attention. She's not gay, but she still left him to befriend me. She found my sense of confidence intriguing. Ever since then, I help her out of her shell and she helps me reel it in. My voice of reason when the inside voices get too loud.

Sam's words sink in slowly. Our last trip together as a group before we all go our separate ways. We've all been friends in one way or another since freshman year in high school. The weirdest fucking Breakfast Club you could imagine. We all contribute something to the group that compliments the others. That never kept us out of trouble, though. I'm honestly impressed any of us are still alive after the childhoods we had. Yet, we're all becoming successful in our young adult years. We've spent the past three years living at home, everyone except Colton forgoing college, to pursue our passions. Each one of us determined to hustle after our dreams. It wasn't until last year that the fruits of our labor started paying off.

Colton was drafted onto the practice team for the Chicago NFL team after attending a junior college for barely two years. He's still expected to finish his Associate's before he could start his contract. Colton didn't mind, though. He saw every opportunity as baby steps to his dream goal of being the captain of a pro-league football team. One day, he'll be on TV and I'll be able to tell everyone, "That's my friend!"

Jason's modeling career picked up pretty quickly after he reigned in his fashion style. He's modeling for whatever the next up-and-coming alternative clothes line is. Creepville? Gothiccc? Black Heart? I don't even know anymore. It's hard to keep count. He talks about it enough that I started to tune him out from time to time. I can only take so many renditions of his stories about being hit on by the staff before I feel physically nauseous.

Sam started her own garden after high school and grew it into the town's first apothecary. It's essentially a holistic shop that focuses on natural remedies, but she still insists on Western medicine for things beyond her control. Lots of people were skeptical about the practice at first. It gained popularity when they realized modern medicine comes from the Earth's most basic ingredients. To her, holistic medicine isn't just woo-woo. It's connecting back to nature in a way science has forgotten.

I used all the dark thoughts inside my head and my obsession with true crime to become Graveslake's first published writer. I'm still considered an Indie author, but I make enough to be self-sustaining without a secondary job. It was the perfect way to channel all those urges inside that I tucked away for good keeping. If anyone asks why I am the way I am, I just point to my writings. You can't really argue with written art.

I turn my gaze back out the window, but keep my attention on the current conversation buzzing through the car. Jason and Sam continue to argue the semantics of a masked serial killer roaming the backwoods of Graveslake as the cabin comes into view. Rumor has it, the killings started back with one of the early 2000's senior class traditions at Graveslake High. A tradition every year to celebrate graduating was to play senior assassin. It's exactly how it sounds. There's the game master who keeps track of the assassin list, collects the money, and rewards the jackpot to the winner. People put money in the pot and get their first "kill". The objective is to catch the assigned kill person by surprise and soak them with a water gun (or other fluids, some sick fucks like to bend the rules). The only off-limits spots were school grounds and the person's place of work. The game continues until the last person stands and the prize is awarded. Some years the game was played well after graduation.

The year the killer arrived, people stopped playing. Within a three week period, ten kids went missing only to slowly have their bodies show up in the woods. They were mutilated beyond anyone's wildest imagination. The crime scene photos were a sadist's wet dream. Those images are seared into my memory. I can slum it with the roughest crime scene journalist, but even this was grotesque.

Mackenzie Fuller's crime scene in particular has stuck in the rumor mill for years. Her body was found skinned and dismembered in the woods behind her house. The corpse was re-articulated postmortem to look like a marionette doll. There was a six inch cavity in her chest that was hollowed out and lined with her skin. Forensic reports showed remnants of latex and glycerin, suggesting the killer used her corpse as his personal flesh light. They didn't find any DNA at the scene. From the police reports and local news, the only thing left behind was a distressed skull mask with the words *time to die* carved into the forehead. This dude went full *movie slasher* with a side of *what the fuck*. The discovery made three veteran cops quit the force on the spot. That was over twenty years ago. Since then, every year one senior disappears right before graduation, rightfully dubbing the mystery killer *The Senior Slayer*. The missing bodies are found months later, mutilated in the same M.O. as the original killing spree. Each year mimicking one of the original ten slayings. After the first ten years, the style of killings reverts back to the beginning. The horrific ritual starts all over again. Last I checked, there's still no DNA traces and no suspects. It leaves the town officials stumped.

Each year, students wonder who will be the unlucky person. Social status doesn't matter to this killer. One year a cheerleader was grabbed. Two years later, the resident dweeb was kidnapped. In our graduating class, the valedictorian was the unlucky victim. He was found four months later at the bottom of the lake. The body was too decomposed to formally connect it to The Senior Slayer, but everyone knew better. It's the dark tradition of our small town. We scheduled our vacation well past graduation and we've been alumni for over three years now. Surely, there's no masked killer still running around in the woods.

I mull over that last thought. I wouldn't be opposed to a masked man arriving for some fun. Being stalked by a ghost is thrilling. It wouldn't be the first time, either. The tingles running down your body when your nerves are on edge. Your breath becomes short and labored. You don't know if you're going to cry or moan in fear. Ugh, that shit makes me wet just thinking about it. And don't even look at me with that face. I told you earlier I like things extra dark. Think I wrote all these horrmance novels without a little...experimenting? People will try the damnedest things given the opportunity. It's fuck or get fucked in this twisted world. I will always choose the latter, thank you.

"We're here!" Colton cheers in the driver seat as he shifts the car into park. His family estate looms in front of us between the oak trees. This cabin was always our summer getaway before school started. It allowed us to exist without expectations or prying parental eyes. This summer, the trip is a little heavier. It's our final get together before we officially go our separate ways into our adult careers. I glance at the clock on the car dash. *1:37 p.m.* We have a whole seventy-two hours to make lasting memories. I send up a silent prayer to the universe hoping this won't be the last time I see my friends. I mean, come on. All the horror movies aside that say you should never be alone in the woods, what's the worst that could happen?

TIME TO DIE

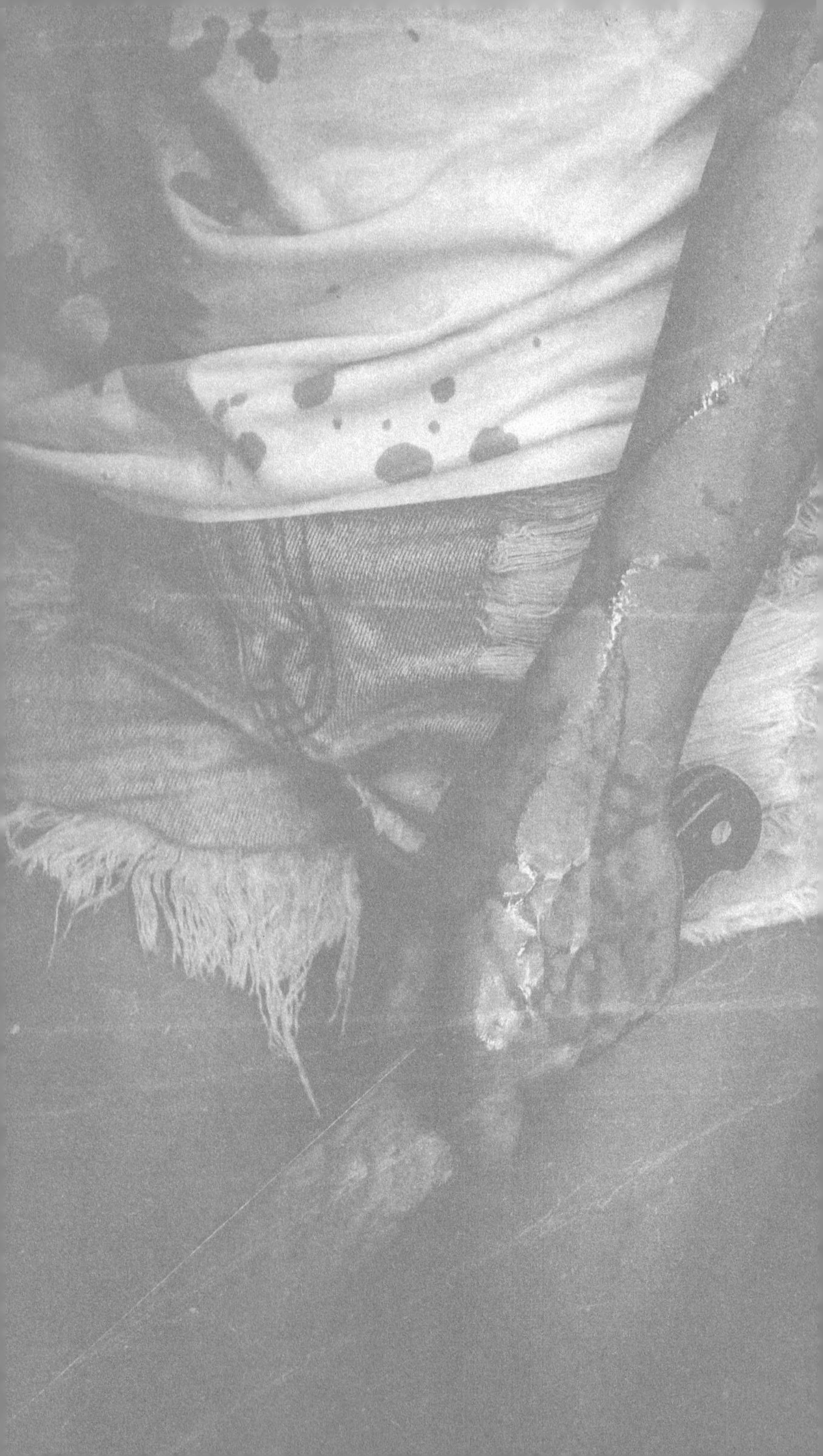

TWO

"**H**ome sweet home, y'all!" Colton throws the front door open with dramatic flare, like it's the first time we've ever seen this place before.

We all follow Colton inside the cabin. It's more of a modern house on a cliff than a cabin. Colton's family inherited this land from his great grandfather, a founder of Graveslake. The original house still exists somewhere on the property. I've never personally seen it, but he claims it's haunted. According to Colton, his parents didn't like vacationing in something so "primitive" and "run down". So, they moved the driveway and built a brand new home overlooking the lake, instead. The house clings to the side of the cliff with a fully furnished balcony. It would make the best location for a secluded horror movie. This building may or may not have been the setting for a few of my earlier writings. It was easy to pull inspiration from here since this was our second home growing up.

"I'm really going to miss this place. The love and memories we filled in this place make it so magical. We love you, Miss Cabin. Only good vibes this weekend." Sam wanders around the room, her rosy, tanned arms outstretched in a greeting to the home. She always starts our trip with a little positive manifestation. I don't really believe in all that stuff, but if it brings her joy, I'm happy to play along.

"Yes, Universe. Please make this the best weekend of our lives. We accept whatever you bring into our space."

Walking over to Sam, I take her hand in mine, mimicking her stance. My hands raise to the sky like a silent prayer. Sam squeezes my hand as she closes her eyes. I can see her start her deep breathing to cement the mantra in her head. This is one of the very few times I see her in her element. Completely calm. She looks so serene and content in this moment. It's honestly kind of beautiful. I admire her from the side as my eyes roam over her body. My breath catches as her perky tits rise up and down beneath her lavender crop top. Her lips part as her breath slows. I know she's not into me, but what I wouldn't give to feel those lips on mine. I blanch at the thought of it and immediately dismiss it. She may be the only girl that holds my attention right now, however, I would never betray her trust like that. Her friendship is more important than a potential fling.

I have enough boys lining up to experience the infamous rumors spread about me to keep myself occupied. It was fun for the first few months when my stories were gaining momentum on BookTok. All these silly "alpha males" sliding into my messages, thinking they can tame the demons inside me. When push came to shove though, they were groveling at my knees. I like them strapped to my bed, spread eagle, a ball gag in their mouth, and a knife to their throat as I ride them, using their small drops of blood as lube until I find my release. Then I let them go on their merry way to finish themselves off at home like the good little fucktoys they are.

No one ever expects the pretty horror writer to actually enjoy the things she writes about. Jokes on them; that's the only way I get off. Writing is my own personal form of foreplay. Maybe one day I can find someone who can match my demented games. I just want one person to fuck me into submission. Chase me down in the woods. Grab me by the throat and throw me like they hate me. Gag and restrain me. Make me fear for my life. Degrade me to the point I'm begging them to fuck my pulsating, wet pussy for sweet release. Treat me like I'm their own little fucktoy. For now, I'll settle for the simps. It's good for PR, anyway. There's no better promotion than self promotion, even if the tactics are less than acceptable to community standards.

"Allllrightttt. Who wants to join me in the bedroom for some extra curricular activity before we start drinking?" Jason grins at us, wiggling his eyebrows suggestively with a bundle of red rope held in his hand. I know shibari rope when I see it.

I roll my eyes.

Way to ruin the mood, asshole.

"Where the fuck did you get that from?" Sam looks at him, disgusted. She barely tolerates his sexual antics on a regular day. I'm sure she hoped this weekend would be different. Jason never means what he says, at least not around us. He respects our boundaries and usually says shit for the jokes. However, there's a part of me that wouldn't be surprised if he didn't secretly hope pushing enough times would make one (or both) of us cave. Sam would never. After her ex, she vowed to only date soft, masculine men. I don't blame her. She deserves someone who worships at her feet like the forest goddess she is.

"You're such a fucking tool, Jay. Keep your shibari rope at home to use with Jill." I wave him off as I turn for the kitchen. An extra strong rum drink is calling my name. A dark and stormy might do the trick. I'm definitely going to need it if this is how we're starting the trip. *For fuck's sake.* If I wrote romcoms, this weekend would be a treasure trove of material. Maybe I can fantasize killing him in my next novel. Let's see how he likes that joke.

"Ashe, you wound me! I have never slept with Jill Adams. Not without lack of trying, at least. She's pretty committed to her boyfriend," Jason says as he follows me into the kitchen. He saunters over, grabbing the bottle of rum I can't reach on the top shelf.

"Thanks," I say, swiping the bottle from him with a scowl. "I wasn't referring to Adams." I hold up my hand with my fingers extended, wiggling each finger to get my point across. I hold in my giggle, waiting for him to catch the reference.

Jason stares at me. His eyes narrow as the joke sets in, lips thinning into a straight line. I can see his jaw tense for a fraction of a second. Then, the tips of his mouth slightly lift. Suddenly, he's on top of me. Putting the bottle down on the counter, he leans in closer and cages me between his arms. His deep, golden eyes darken when I look up at him, annoyance flooding my veins. There's a flutter from somewhere inside me that awakens. I try to push it back down because this is *Jason*. He's disgusting and I refuse to give him what he wants. Admittedly, I'm failing miserably as the annoyance slowly fades into pulsating desire. He's doing the one thing no one else has been able to do — make me feel help-less and small. I'm only five foot eight, so his six foot five frame easily towers over me. My bitchy attitude usually makes up for what I lack in height, but right now, that atti-tude is only egging him on.

I try to move one of his arms to leave. He grabs my wrist and pins it back to the counter's edge. His other hand plays with a stray strand of blue hair that escaped from behind my ear.

Jason leans in close enough that I can feel his breath against my neck, but not so close for me to feel his lips against my side. Goosebumps rise on my skin. My breath shallows, waiting to see what he's going to do. His whisper is low and deep, rumbling through the most sensitive parts of me. "You think about me jacking off, Ashe? You better watch your words this weekend or I might just find another way to occupy that smart mouth of yours."

He pulls away. A shit eating grin covers his face as he saunters away. I'm left speechless for the first time in history. No witty comeback. No snarky remark about him having a tiny dick. For years, I've been suppressing any urge towards wanting him and for the first time in a long time, I don't feel in control of the situation. That's not how I like to operate. When I'm in control, I know exactly what will happen. I have the power to make the outcome whatever I want.

I'm standing there, looking like an idiot with my mouth gaped open, when I hear Jason's haughty, deep voice echo in from the doorway.

"*Good girl.*"

Did...did he just?

Did he just fucking good girl *me*?!

Gods, have mercy on my black soul.

I hate that my body betrays me. My insides clench while fantasies run wild from that one, little phrase. The idea of Jason pinning me against the wall, feeling his breath on my skin. I catch myself wondering what his hardness would feel like pressed up against me, clawing at his back as he makes me submit to him. A million variations of positions haunt my imagination.

Do I seriously want to fuck Jason Vera?

This weekend is not going to go as expected.

If this is any indication of what's to come, I need to stay on guard. There's no way I'm ending this trip cumming on Jason's dick. Nope. Can't fucking do it. I made a deal with myself. There's some lines I just won't cross.

Colton walks into the kitchen looking back at Jason as he passes, confusion lining his face. I pick my jaw up off the metaphorical floor and return my composure to its natural, resting bitch face before he figures out what's going on. Turning back to the counter, I grab the rum bottle and a glass to start making my drink. The spiced, golden liquid reminds me of the brief interaction that just occurred with matching amber eyes. I shoot a glance at Colton. When he looks back at me, I can tell he's still confused.

"What the fuck was Jason mumbling about?"

"The usual bullshit. He's trying to get underneath my skin." I shrug, finishing my drink I was *so rudely* interrupted in making.

Colton joins me at the counter, grabbing a glass for himself. He grabs some ice from the freezer and returns with a handful for me, as well.

"Thanks!" I say, smiling warmly at my best friend as we clink our glasses. "Cheers!"

Colton takes a swig of what I assume is his expensive whiskey. He really takes this *All-American boy* persona seriously. Below that meathead exterior though, he's actually really calculating when it comes to his career. He has an image to maintain. It's what caught University of Wisconsin's attention during try-outs. He wasn't just a good player, he was also the wet dream of every basic white girl out there. The boy you could bring home to your parents. Someone who could be your Prince Charming. He will always be just Colton to me, though.

We met freshman year in theater. It's not something he publicly shares. Very few jocks were in the fine arts department, let alone excelled at it. We were paired to do a comedy scene together. He was wary of me at first. In high school, I went way overboard into the emo-scene trend. The raccoon tail, colored hair, all black clothes, dark makeup, and brooding expressions. Unless you really got to know me, I was just that "bitchy emo girl". We became best friends when Colton realized the fashion was only skin deep, my dark humor was borderline certifiable, and I cursed like a Marine. He told me once he likes the fact I treat him like a human instead of just eye candy. Who knew a jock could have a heart *and* a brain?

"Are you ready for training to start?" I ask him. Practice team isn't exactly something to write home about, but it's still a big deal in the grand scheme of his career. It's the stepping stone to a bigger position in the future. I know he'll take it just as seriously as if he was at a starting line.

Colton nods as he finishes his first drink.

"I think so. The coaches sent me over a nutrition guide to start on Monday before we officially start. I know that practice team isn't my forever gig, but it'll give me time to learn the tricks of the trade. I'll make enough so I won't have to worry about money and can solely focus on strengthening my skills. I'm really grateful I got this chance to do something bigger than me." Always the humble Colton. I smile at him warmly. I'm going to miss these sweet moments we share.

"You're going to do great, Colt. I can't wait to see you on national TV one day and cheer for my best friend kicking the other team's ass!" I wrap him in a reassuring hug. Just because I write horror and like to degrade people, doesn't mean I can't have a soft side. I genuinely care about the people closest to me. I want them to be happy. Colton returns the embrace with the biggest bear hug. He picks me up off the ground, squeezing my insides until I can't breathe.

"Okay, big boy. Put me down before you break me in half," I choke out. He chuckles before letting me go.

"Thank you, Ashe. I promise I won't forget you when I make it big. I love you, bitch." He taps me on the shoulder with his fist.

"I love you, too, jerk," I say, returning his jab with a little more force.

Our gentle moment is cut short. The scream of a dying banshee fills the room.

It stops just as quickly as it started.

Then everything goes silent.

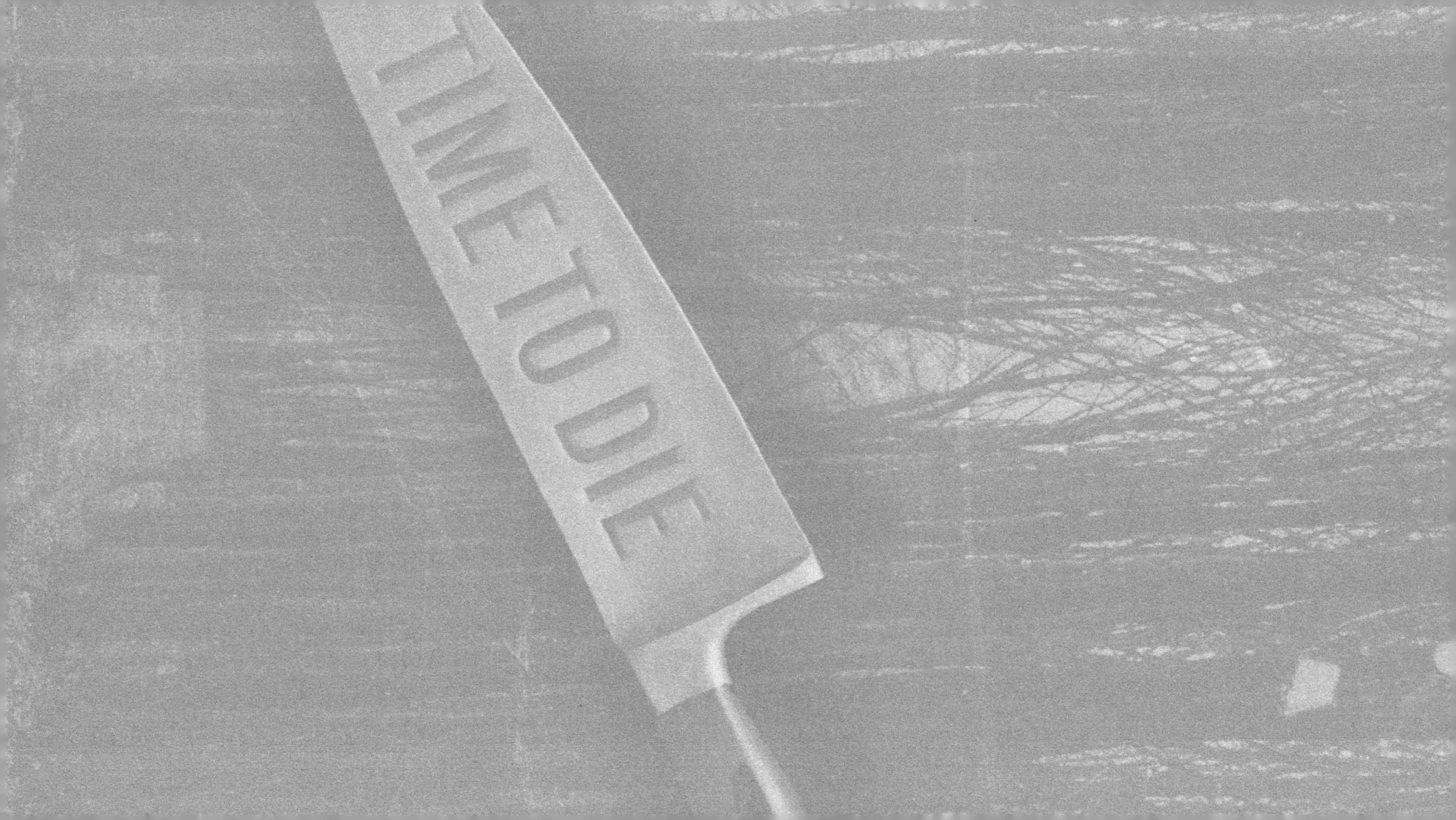

TIME TO DIE

THREE

Colton and I rush out of the kitchen towards the blood curdling scream we just heard. The accordion glass door to the balcony is open as Sam sits in the shade on her tie-dye yoga mat. Her arms are covering her eyes to avoid looking in front of her. We hear every explicit flow from her mouth.

"Fucking hell. You're such a goddamn dickhead, Jason. I hope you get ass fucked by a cactus. Screw you!"

Colton and I stare at each other. *What did we miss in the last five minutes?*

I look over to the deck elevator behind us. Jason is doubled over in laughter, butt ass naked. Everything is showing in the sun. I do my best to not linger too long on his toned body, but it's long enough for me to notice what he's packing below the belt. I quickly glance away and feel a red blush creep over my face. My question from earlier has definitely been answered. I mentally think of dead puppies and wrinkly, old man balls to calm my racing thoughts.

Gods be damned. I knew Jason was always an arrogant prick, I just didn't know he had the cock to prove it. He's clearly a shower and not a grower, but I'm not complaining about it. What would he look like aroused? The thought makes my insides flutter again. I groan at the mental image. This is *not* fucking helping my case to avoid getting in his bed this weekend. I take three deep breaths before heading towards Sam.

Colton is already handing Jason a towel with the most disapproving frown on his face. I can't hear what they're saying. I can only imagine Colton is ripping him a new one for his exploits in broad day light.

Sam has calmed down a bit by the time I reach her. It's not the first time Jason has pulled this stunt. He's notorious for skinny dipping during our visits. I'm all for body positivity, but come on, man! Have some decency when the sun is still up. I sit next to Sam and rest my head on her shoulder. A gesture of good faith. I'm on her side for this one, no matter how much my kitty wants to know how he feels slipping inside me.

No. Fucking stop, Ashe.

I push the thought away again.

"You good, girl?" I ask her as we watch the boys descend in the elevator.

Colton waves at us like the clown from that Stephen King movie. His disappointment is now replaced with a mischievous grin. Whatever annoyance he felt before is long gone. I mentally take note to check the kayaks later before using them. It wouldn't be the first time Sam or I have found a hoard of spiders inside, cleverly placed by Colton or Jason to watch us squirm like little girls. I may have an obsession with horror, but creepy crawlies is where I draw the line. It gives me the literal ick.

My eye darts to the other side of the elevator before it descends out of view. Jason is staring directly at us. Well, directly at *me*. He's leaning against the back wall of the elevator, casually holding onto the back railing with his head tilted to the side. His towel is wrapped dangerously low on his waist as he watches me. Waiting for a reaction. My breath catches and my body freezes under his gaze. I can feel a blush creeping up my neck. Every nerve in my body is on fire. The burning desire I felt earlier returns with a vengeance. I'm hyper aware of my eyes widening when my brain finally catches up with what my body already knows. Somehow, someway, I want to fuck Jason. Jason's eyes flash in response. He knows the effect he's having on me. The same smoldering smirk on his face that I saw earlier in the kitchen makes another appearance as he moves out of view.

"Ugh. Jason can be such an ass sometimes. Totally ruined the vibe for my chakra meditation. I was trying to get in the right head space and now all I can think of is his head. In my face." Sam shudders, dramatically trying to get the *ick* off her body and mind.

"Yeah," I say casually, stuck staring at the spot Jason disappeared from view. "You have to admire his confidence, though."

Silence falls through the space between us. I continue staring at the spot. I'm highly aware of what I just said. Maybe if I don't acknowledge what was said, then it won't be a big deal. Sam is my best friend, though. She knows everything about me, so she definitely knows what's going through my head right now.

I can feel Sam's stare burning into the side of my face. I

take a hesitant glance towards her. Her face is contorted into the most extreme side eye in existence.

"Excuseeeee me. Earth to Ashe! Is that really you in there? You just gave Jason a compliment. He's not even here and it wasn't followed up by a snarky joke."

My mind races to find an excuse as to why in the world I would say something nice about Jason. It's not that I hate him, but that's how our relationship has always been. He pushes my buttons. I tell him to fuck off. Then I get back at him with a stupid prank. It usually involves some level of grotesque gore or humiliation. The last time he pissed me off, I super glued a King Dong to the hood of his truck. It took him a week to pry it off. Round and round the cycle we go. Anything to avoid whatever feelings might be lingering beneath the games.

Jason joined the group midway through freshman year. Sam, Colton, and I were the trio no one expected to see in school. The hippy, the jock, and the horror girl. Our love of music and books brought us together. We bonded over our childhoods, the realization that we weren't alone in this twisted world kept us together.

Colton was already friends with Jason before he met us. He brought Jason to a few gatherings. He wasn't officially accepted into the group until he came to a rave we had planned. Sam and I learned who Jason truly was that night. Even though his appearance was a shy, emo boy knockoff, Jason's personality made up for it in droves. He made dick jokes the entire time driving there. Sam was ready to snap his neck by the time we got to the venue, which means something fierce coming from the resident *make love, not war* girl. I secretly found it amusing, but I refused to let him know that. I had an image to maintain. Each joke was met with an equally sarcastic quip from me. It was invigorating to finally have someone match me verbally, blow for blow. Back and forth we went that night, participating in what I could only describe as linguistic foreplay. That was until the headliner music started. Jason changed. We could visibly see him melt away into the beat. He knew every single damn beat and pantomimed the most dramatic scenes while dancing. It was endearing to see someone who's usually so high energy surrender to the music. We screamed our hearts out, danced together, and went apeshit with each new song. There was a single moment where I could have sworn Jason was going to kiss me.

It was towards the end of the night. We had all been drinking and taking hits off the joint Sam snuck into the venue. It was the final song and I was swaying with the music. Jason grabbed my hand, swinging me into him. We waltzed together, laughing to the song. When I looked up at him, I saw it. The lust in his eyes as he peered down at me. I felt his warm arms wrap tighter around my waist. He pulled me closer. Our lips were mere inches apart. I could smell the mixture of sweet rum and pineapple on his breath. In a lapse of better judgment, I leaned in to close the distance. The song ended before our lips met. He immediately released me, acting as if we weren't seconds away from sucking each other's faces off. I awkwardly took a step back and wrapped my arms around myself, ignoring the embarrassment creeping across my face. Of course, he wouldn't actually kiss me. This was Jason we were talking about; crude, mildly disrespectful, and a little unhinged. Definitely not something I wanted to entangle myself with.

Now, though? I can't even form a coherent thought with him around. It has to be whatever fuckboy dating tips he picked up while modeling. Falling for the ravened-hair, bad boy is too cliche, even for me.

I shift my legs out in front of me and lean back. I don't have an answer for Sam. She would kill me if she knew the flashback I was having right now.

"Do you want to go kayaking once you're done meditating?" I ask her as nonchalantly as possible.

"No fucking way. Nope. You're not getting away with it that easily! Answer my question. Did you just give Jason a compliment?"

I shrug, propping my arms up to feel the sun on my face. Maybe I can lie my way out of this. "He's growing on me. We're not going to see each other for a while after this trip. I figured it's time to start being nice to him."

Sam glares at me. She can see straight through my bullshit. She knows damn well that I'm lying right now. Hopefully, I did it well enough that she'll leave it alone.

"Uh huh. Sure. Let's go with that. It has nothing to do with the interaction you guys had in the kitchen earlier?"

I bolt upright. My skin is ice cold. There's no fucking way she saw or heard anything that happened in the kitchen earlier. I vowed to take that to the grave. I was so sure no one saw what happened between Jason and I.

I'm certain she can feel the anxiety rolling off my body.

"Wh-what happened in the kitchen?"

Sam laughs. "Denial is a river in Egypt, babe. Don't think I didn't see Jason trying to seduce you on my way to go mediate. He basically had you in the palm of his hands. You were straight up giving him *fuck me* eyes."

I say nothing. She's right. I have no way to talk myself out of this. "I wasn't actually going to sleep with him. He picked up some weird Jedi mind tricks while modeling and he thought he could convince me into bed."

"Ashe, I'm not going to tell you whose disco stick you can and cannot take a ride on. I know the shit you get into on your book tours. You've told me. All I ask is that you keep yourself and your soul safe. You, me, this group; we're more important than some crazy weekend fling. I don't want you to lose a friend because you started thinking with lust instead of logic. Keep that in mind next time Master Jason tries his mind tricks on you." Sam hugs me. Her touch is gentle and comforting. I return the hug, breathing in her perfume of candied vanilla spice. She's right. I know better than to ruin a good thing. I know it's just my lack of excitement in the bedroom lately. Still, the chaos gremlin in the back of my mind wants to know what it would feel like if I gave in.

I release her, thankful for the pep talk. Sam never judges me, but she definitely puts me in my place when need be.

"I'm going to go pack a lake bag. Finish up your meditation, we can go find the boys in a bit. I want some lake time before dinner." I smile at her as I get up.

Sam returns to her mat and settles into child's pose. I hear her yell at me over my shoulder, "You better have packed a moo-moo in that bag of yours or Jason is going to be a lot harder to ignore this weekend." I chuckle, she's such an asshole sometimes.

It's mid-day and the sun is blistering overhead. The humidity clings to my skin, making it damp and sticky. It's damn near impossible to cool off by sweating alone and, right now, I'm covered in it. Perfect time to hop in the water. Sam and I find the boys on the dock. They're already set up for fishing, a beer cooler between them, and folding lawn chairs on each side of the dock. A small duffle bag overflowing with discarded clothes sits next to the cooler. Colton has ditched his shirt for a black pair of swim trunks with sharks eating donuts. He's posed in his chair ready for a nap with the rod tucked safely between his legs, hand on the reel ready to pull when he feels a tug.

Jason wears a black tank top with a matching pair of black swim trunks. The tank is skin tight, showing off every ripple of ink and muscle Jason has acquired over the past three years. He's not the boy we met in high school, anymore. I remember he started lifting around the same time he started taking his fashion seriously. He stated it was to get a better chance of getting signed by a talent agency. It worked. He's now the face of every independent alternative magazine and clothing company. I watch as he reaches down to grasp the fishing rod with his right hand. The way the muscles in his forearm constrict when he grasps the pole makes me daydream what his hand would look like wrapped around my neck.

Everything inside me is screaming. My mind continues to wonder about all the dirty things I would let Jason do to me. My eyes follow the bulging vein in his forearm up to his broad shoulders. His chest is chiseled like a superhero. After the incident in the kitchen today, I'm confident he could probably pick up my curvy frame. My eyes flicker to his face and he's watching me again, knowingness lingering in his eyes. He winks at me before turning to his chair and sits down without another glance. Again, I'm left defenseless and sexually frustrated. He should *not* have this effect on me. It's not like I've had a dry spell recently, all the current simps just don't do anything for me. It's so boring being worshiped all the time, and to be completely honest, most of them can't find the clit with a well drawn map.

Sam breaks my inward spiral.

"Ashe, wanna go kayaking?" She's looking at me through narrow eyes. It's like she can read my mind. I blanch in response and mentally wipe the drool from my face. *I'm so fucked this weekend.* Literally. Jason is going to be my downfall. I quickly shake my head to remove any other dirty thoughts and square my shoulders.

"You better check the haul first. I bet you $20 Colton put a dead squirrel in there for us to find." I send a pointed look to where Colton is sitting.

"I would never do such a thing," Colton mumbles under his hat, not moving from his napping position.

Sam giggles as she walks towards the wooden structure. I roll my eyes and follow her. He's right, it wouldn't be a dead squirrel. That's more in my territory. Still, I'm wary as we open the door to the shed. Sam steps in first, knocking down cobwebs as she finds the light switch. The overhead bulbs flicker to light as the dull buzz of incandescent fills the space. This is the setting of every lake horror movie in existence – you cannot change my mind. We weave through the piles of junk collected over the years until we reach the garage door. Sam unlocks the door and I slide it up until it clicks into place overhead. The clear blue lake invites us into its watery depths.

I turn to help Sam pull down the two orange kayaks from the ceiling. The first one slips out easily from the hooks it rests on, but the second one gets stuck as a hook catches on the lip of the haul opening. We both shimmy and pull the kayak until it comes tumbling down on top of us. A small yelp escapes Sam's lips while I'm laughing underneath the kayak before we roll it off. A small clinking sound rattles around the inside of the kayak. We look at each other. Sam jiggles the front of the kayak. The rattling persists. There's definitely something inside that shouldn't be there.

"I fucking told you the guys were going to mess with us," I whine as I watch Sam grab one of the paddles from the wall.

"It could be a screw or an old beer can. Don't be so negative, Ashe. Happy thoughts. Put happiness into the universe." Sam takes the paddle and digs inside the kayak. She's digging for a few seconds before the paddle catches on something. She starts pulling the paddle out with whatever is stuck inside scraping against the bottom. Once the paddle is out, Sam picks up the kayak and flips it over. A dirty skull mask drops out of the opening and lands directly between us on the floor.

Sam drops the kayak and neither one of us speaks. Neither one of us moves from our place on the ground. We've seen that mask before.It's been plastered all over the news for most of our lives. When everyone started disappearing. When Mackenzie was found. There's no denying what's in front of us. Despite similar masks being sold every year for costumes during Halloween, this one is different. Anyone who knows about the Graveslake murders knows the killer's signature calling card wasn't just a skull, it was personalized. Crudely carved into the forehead of the mask and painted with dried blood was a deadly promise: *time to die*. That same phrase is right in front of us.

The haunting, empty eyes stares back at us.

TIME TO DIE

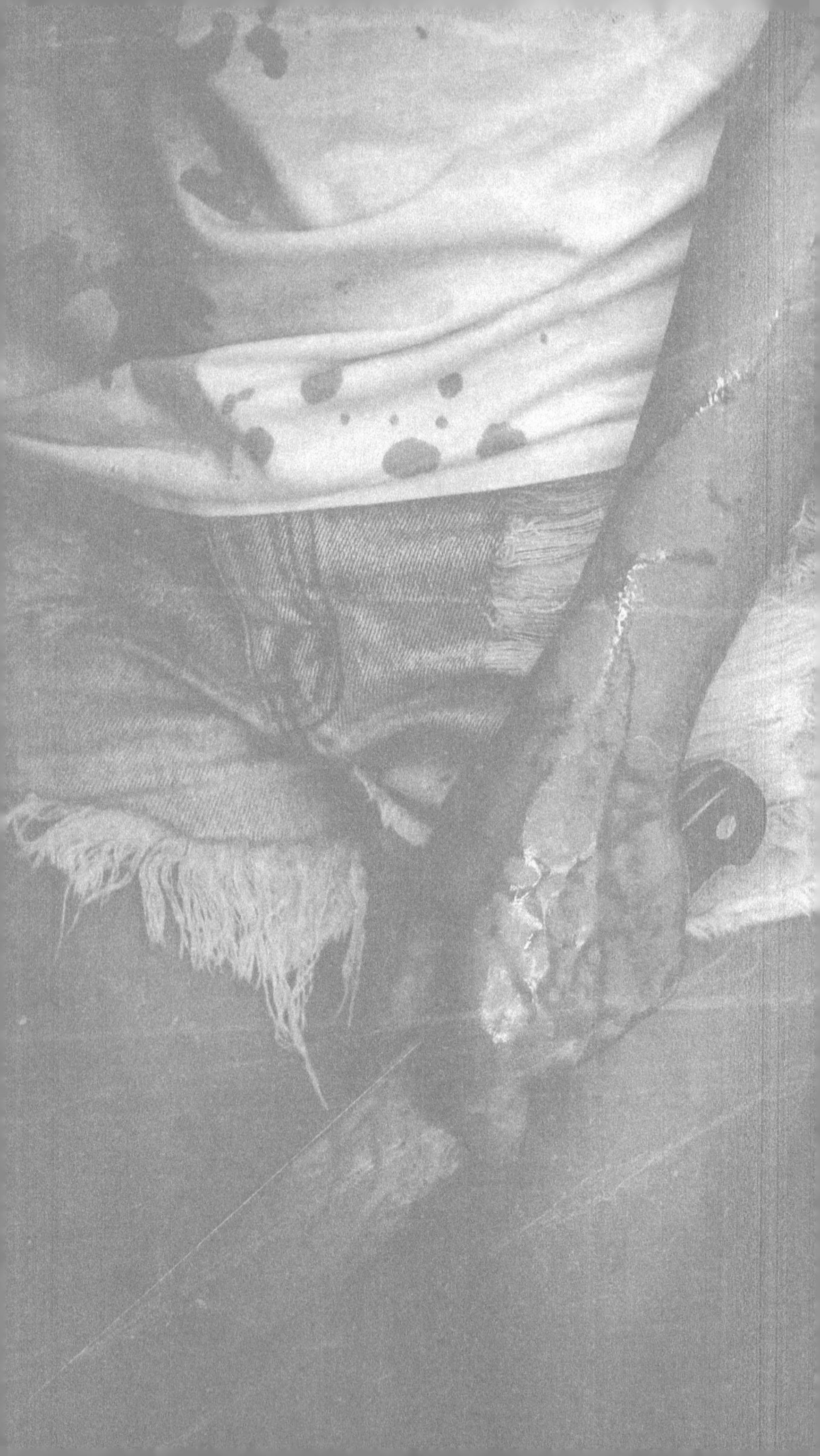

FOUR

Sam is in a fury, running out of the shed with the mask in hand. I barely catch up to her before she's chucking the mask at the boys. It hits Jason square in the back of the head. She's fuming.

"Bro, what the fuck was that?" Jason coddles his head where the object made contact. He gets out of his lawn chair to turn towards a very angry Sam. The mask lies between Colton and Jason on the dock.

"You think this is fucking funny?!" Sam points to the damning evidence between them.

Jason follows Sam's finger to the spot she's pointing on the dock and his body goes rigid. I watch his face as a wide array of emotions run through his mind until anger is the one he lands on. When he looks back up at Sam, his eyes are heated.

"You *really* think I would prank you guys like that? Joke

about all those seniors who didn't make it to graduation. I'm crude, sure, but I'm not that demented, Sam. This is how you think of your friends?" Jason demands. He's not yelling, but I know he wants to. He's raging underneath that calm demeanor, both hands clenched at his side as evidence. His knuckles are white with how tightly he's digging his fingers into his palms.

Sam turns up her nose at him. I know that look – she doesn't believe him. "Sorry, not sorry. I don't believe you."

See? Told you.

"After all those photo shoots you've done recently with GoTHICC clothing line at The Baphomet Temple, maybe you picked up a few messed up ideas."

"Fuck you, Sam. You know damn well TBT doesn't actually believe in Satan or evil. *Ashe* is the horror freak. *She's* the one who takes pranks too far. Why don't you ask her?!"

If I could roll my eyes any deeper into my skull, I would. Of course, he's going to try to change the subject. Placing blame on me is easy, except for the fact I haven't been down here yet this trip.

"I haven't even been down here today until now. How the hell would I be able to plant that?" I cross my arms as I stare at him. Let's see how he talks his way out of this one.

Jason's silent. He unclenches his hands and crosses his sculpted arms across his chest, his lips pursed in a thin line. He's clearly thinking of a better excuse to give us. Sam and I stare back at him waiting for an answer.

It feels like minutes tick by. Everyone sitting in silence waiting for one of us to break. A showdown to see who's going to own up to this fucked up prank.

Colton speaks up before one of us cracks, breaking the silence the only way he knows best.

"Either go have a weird, hate-fuck threesome or get

over it. It's our last trip. It's really not that bad." He's sitting up now in his lawn chair. His hat is placed back on his head as he looks at us. The disapproving look has returned.

"That is one way to settle this. Ladies?" Jason raises his eyebrow at us and holds his arms out. An invitation for something neither Sam or I would accept.

I scoff at him dramatically. What is this? Some weird reality show on MTV? That would literally never happen.

"Hard pass there, skippy."

Sam scrunches her nose in disgust for the second time this weekend, her face turning into a permanent frown. She crosses her arms and starts pouting. This didn't go the way she wanted.

"I would rather get back with my ex before getting in the bed with you, Jason."

Jason smiles wildly. "That's your stipulation? I can find his number and make that happen. Last I heard, he's still obsessing over the fact you left him to become friends with Ashe. He thinks you're secretly together and, if that's the case, I want to watch."

"Ugh. Shut up, Jason!" Sam throws her arms up in defeat. The energy surrounding our discovery dissipates and the group dynamic returns to homeostasis.

Colton gets up in front of his seat. He swipes the masks from off the dock and examines it in his hands, flipping it over before putting it over his face. No one has actually seen the killer in real life, but I can only imagine the confusion and fear in someone if they saw this haunting face chasing after them. Colton is a big dude, too. Even a seasoned freak like myself would probably hesitate for a second in disbelief before running for my life. Colton dramatically jumps at us. Sam jumps back and screams. Jason flinches. I just stand there, laughing at his antics. It's cute.

Colton chuckles as he removes the mask. "I was wondering what you were doing in the shed for so long. This is a good replica, Jason. How'd you get the words to stay so red? It looks fresh."

Jason throws his hands in the air and gestures towards Colton. "I told you guys. It wasn't me. I assumed you planted it there when you came up last weekend to clean up."

Colton shakes his head as he hands the mask to Jason. Jason brings the cursed thing near his face, examining the letters closer.

"Nah, man. I didn't even check the shed when I came last weekend," Colton says.

Jason frowns again. He's silent for a minute, deep in thought. I'm watching him again, wondering what's going on in his beautiful head. His finger swipes at one of the letters on the forehead. It comes away stained red. He looks up at us; his face ghost white.

"Stop with the dramatics, Jason," I chastise him. Clearly, they added the paint before they hid the mask earlier. Even if they deny it, I know for a fact it was one of them.

Jason shakes his head and passes the mask towards me. "It isn't paint, Ashe."

I yank the object away from him, inspecting the letters for myself. My fingers trace over the maroon carvings.

"What the fuck do you mean it's not–" I halt as I bring my fingers to my nose and the smell hits me. Metallic and earthy notes hang in the air in front of me. Everything in me is on high alert. I know that smell all too well.

Blood.

My index finger drags across the T in *time*. I hold it up to the sky to see it better. The red liquid clings to my finger.

It's sticky and slightly translucent in the sunlight. What kind of blood, I don't know, but it's unmistakably blood.

"Call the cops," I mumble. It's barely a whisper. I'm unable to tear my eyes away from my finger. My overactive imagination is running through every plausible reason as to why this mask has *blood* on it and none of them are comforting.

"Call the cops!" I yell at the group.

FIVE

We're all sitting in the living room of the cabin as we wait for the cops to arrive. The infamous mask lays between us on the oversize, metal coffee table at the center of the room. No one wants to talk, especially to me. Silence ripples through the space between us, each one of us spiraling through our own dark thoughts.

Colton is sitting in the leather love seat in front of the fireplace. He's bent over, his face in his hands. He hasn't spoken a word since he got off the phone with the police. Every once in a while I see his shoulders shake. I can't tell whether it's heavy breathing to calm himself or if he's silently crying.

Sam is on the couch at the head of the room. She's buried deep in a fuzzy, black blanket. Soft sobs come from her direction. She's handling it the worst out of all of us. She went into a full blown panic attack when we realized the mask could be real. It took both boys to drag her up to the cabin for safety.

Am I next?! I was the one who found the mask. We can't be. We survived senior year! This isn't fair! I don't want to die. I can't. I have too much work to do. I have my mom. She wouldn't be able to handle me gone. I can't leave her! I can't!

For what feels like the first time in history, Jason is quiet. No dirty jokes. No crude remarks. He's sitting on the other end of the couch like a statue. He hasn't taken his eyes off of me since we got inside. It makes me uneasy. This isn't the same lustful stare I got earlier from him, this is darker. More accusing and sinister. Like he's hiding something...or he thinks *I'm* hiding something. His hands are resting on his thighs. Occasionally, I can see his fingers twitch, like he wants to grab me by my throat and shove me against the wall until he gets answers. That would be an interesting way to pass the time while we wait; I'm not even going to lie. It's better than the awkward stillness we're sitting in now.

I already tried reasoning with the group. Sure, I love gore and guts, but why in the world would I stage this as a prank? I'm still respectful of the trauma that infects this town like a plague. It's hard to ignore when we're reminded of the Slayer's killings constantly. Every year, a curfew is created for the six weeks before graduation. Every year, the school reminds the graduating class that the senior assassin game is banned from school grounds, quoting they don't want to tempt the killer further. Every year, police presence is magnified in public spaces. Yet, every year, one senior still goes missing. Every year, I honor the fallen by adding another installment to my horror romance collection and updating the crime database for the local newspaper.

The police department tried to argue at one point that my earlier books were reckless since they contained so much information about the original killings. They went so far as to accuse me of newer murders because I have such an intimate knowledge of how to recreate the Slayer's iconic kill scenes. Which, fair, because I was able to dig up information most civilians wouldn't be able to find, but that was a form of therapy for me. Hell, it was cheaper than therapy and actually made me money in return. I couldn't get any other stories on paper until I got the town's story, *secretly my story*, out of my mind. The first book was more of a dramatized non-fiction. Since I was the only one brave enough, or crazy, depending on who you ask, to write about our town's history, it blew up. The local press for that release was ridiculous.

"Graveslake Resident Reveals All of Town's Secrets"

"Rumors Spread About New Author's Connection to Slayer"

"Ashe Nikko Has a Death Wish: What You Need to Know About the Killer New Author"

I was promoting my writings on Instagram and TikTok. For a whole month, all anyone wanted from me was my process for writing that book. My following grew from 500 to 500,000 overnight. That might not seem a lot for the average social influencer, but that's a big market for an Indie author who's just starting out. I talked about the slayings so much I became numb to the topic. I could recite every crime scene in detail. I knew every victim by name. Even though everyone was always asking for me details on the killer, I made sure to keep the victims front and center. They deserved to be remembered. That's how I would want to be remembered if the killer had his way with me. I never told a soul about the event that changed my life senior year. I almost became a Senior Slayer victim myself.

I was on my way home from the library one night after a grueling study session. It was spring and finals were a week away. All anyone cared about was graduating...and surviving. Whispers of the Senior Slayer's return drifted through the town. Everyone knew the killing was inevitable. It was just a matter of when and who. Most seniors kept in packs towards the end of the year, safety in numbers and all that. I was cocky enough, or stupid enough, to think I was immune to falling victim. As the resident crime junkie, I was confident I could survive on my own. I had been preparing for this my whole life.

My cockiness almost got me killed.

2 YEARS EARLIER

The night is brisk with the faint smell of blooming flowers in the distance. The promise of a new beginning and warm Summer nights hang in the air. The sun just set when the library locked up for the night. Crickets chirp in the distance as I quickly make my way to my car. I was almost ready to unlock my door when the hairs on the back of my neck prickled. I freeze. My intuition had never steered me wrong before. My ears strain to hear something or someone off in the distance. Dread bubbles in the pit of my stomach as the atmosphere becomes eerily quiet. Even the crickets stopped their nighttime serenade.

Something zings by my face and made contact with the driver side window. The glass shattered into a melodic cascade of sparkling shards. I scramble to reach for my taser in my backpack. I feel my hand wrap around the device when a warmness creeps up behind me. Strong hands cover my eyes. The scent of leather seeps into my nostrils. I try to scream, but it's muffled by a gag being shoved into my mouth. Coarse fibers scratch across my tongue and rub my lips raw at the contact. Arms and legs flail against my capture, anything to try to break free. Screams continued to flow from my throat until I'm hoarse. My mouth strained against the gag. I can feel my lungs start to hyperventilate. The lack of air make my attempts to escape weaker with each struggle, tears pooling in my eyes clouding my vision.

I'm the true crime fanatic. The weird girl who was intrigued by death. How could I be so stupid to think I couldn't be a target? I wanted so badly to be a final girl that I made myself a target. I mentally berate myself as the killer drags me away to what I could only assume was the woods behind the library. Sticks snap under our feet and leaves crinkle around us as we push deeper into the woods. Grunts escape from the unknown person behind me as I continue to thrash against their hold. Time moves slowly. Each minute feels like an eternity while I wait for my fate. We stop after what felt like a mile of trekking through the woods.

My captor throws me to the ground against a tree. My head makes contact with the rough trunk with a deadening thud, leaving me stunned. Tree bark bites into my right cheek and upper lip, exposing the soft tissue underneath. Blood quickly begins welling up from the cuts. Warm, sticky wetness trickles to the ground beneath me. Before I can process what is happening, a steel-toed shoe makes contact with my stomach. I wheeze as the wind gets knocked out of me. Coughs erupt from the gag as I try to catch my breath. Another blow makes contact to my rib cage. The distinct crack of a bone is deafening in the silence of the woods. A guttural scream rips through me as I clutch my side.

I lay there in the fetal position, trying to cover the most intimate parts of my body being exposed to the assault. Suddenly, a hand wraps around the back of my head. The assailant grips a fistful of hair, holding me upright. The gag is swiftly ripped from my face, leaving my mouth raw from the fabric. I blink away tears as I look up at my torturer. A mask covers his features, similar to The Senior Slayer, but his body is familiar. He crouches down, removing the bloodied mask and revealing his true face. It takes a second for my brain to register who is standing in front of me. I blink a few times, expecting them to disappear like a bad dream.

"Tristan?" I rasp out.

Tristan is one of the sweetest guys in our grade. I only had a few classes with him, but our school was small. Everyone knows everyone in some way. He's the president of our high school's Honor Society and set to be our valedictorian. He's seen every weekend volunteering at the local animal shelter. A church-going, good boy. Someone any parent would be proud to see their child dating. Someone no one would assume had these demons crawling inside poisoning his mind.

Tristan transforms as a devilish smirk spreads across his face with my realization. He tightens his grip on the back of my head, making me whimper in pain. My head makes contact with the tree again as he slams me against the trunk. I crumble as the air forcefully leaves my body. I start gasping for breath. He chuckles at my torment.

"You're not the killer, Tristan," I plead with him. "You're

a good kid. Just walk away. I won't tell if you let me go. I promise."

Tristan peers at me with a blank stare. His eyes are dark as he watches me try to regain my strength. I fight with his hand against the back of my head as I try to break free. Tristan forces me upright, dragging my back against the rough bark. Each inch slices a new cut into the flesh on my back. Blood soaks through my shirt and I can feel the warm liquid drip down my legs.

Standing face to face, Tristan releases his grip. He walks a few paces away before turning back to me. My body is frozen, but my mind continues to race thinking of a way to escape.

"That's the thing, Ashe. I can't walk away. He's here, you know. The Senior Slayer. He's always been here."

Tristan begins stalking closer to me. I can see the faint glimmer of something metallic in his hand.

"Tristan, please," I begin to plead again. "I know you don't have to do this."

"Oh, but I do. It's a part of the game. Senior Assassin might have ended the year the killer showed up, but he created a new game. All those seniors that have died since? They're a dedication."

"What the fuck do you mean 'a dedication'?" I ask, inching around the tree trunk to find a space to run.

Tristan quickly stands in my way, my legs pinned between his large frame and the hard tree behind me. He raises a knife to my cheek, inspecting the cut that formed from being shoved against the harsh tree bark. The knife plays across the soft skin on my cupid's bow to my other cheek. Without warning, Tristan slices through the tender flesh on the other cheek into a matching cut.

I cry out. My hands instinctively reach to my face to

cover the fresh cut. My fingers sink into the wound with ease. Blood weeps over my hand as I try to close the gap.

"A dedication to *him*. A promise of loyalty. He chooses who is lucky enough to join his game. If you play the game right and follow all the rules, you win the prize. You can walk away like nothing ever happened. Start your adult life with no worries."

"So he pays you to kill people?" I ask, lacing my voice with as much disgust as humanly possible.

Tristan shrugs, never removing the knife from my face. "Something like that."

"That's fucking fantastic. So happy that *you're* the chosen one, Anakin. What about all those seniors who get caught in the cross fire? They didn't ask for this. *I* didn't ask for this!" I spit at him as I tried to shove his massive body. There is no escaping his embrace. His hand flies to my neck. The knife in his other hand moves to rest against my stomach, the tip of the blade poised directly to my belly button. His strong fingers dig into my sensitive skin. He tilts my head up against the tree, causing the bark to bite further, and leans in. His breath is hot and heavy against my neck. He trails his nose up and down my neck as I squirm under his embrace.

"Collateral damage. But it's fucking worth it if you knew what the prize was," he whispers into my ear.

"Then enlighten me," I choke out, probing for an answer. I try to be as still as possible, careful not dig the blade deeper into my abdomen.

Tristan leans back to stare at my contorted body. He removes the knife from my stomach and moves it down to the hem of my shirt. Jerking up, the fabric of my shirt rips through the center in one fluid motion. Cold night air floats over my exposed breasts. I curse myself for choosing to go commando today. Against my will, my nipples harden in response. A deep rumble escapes from Tristan as he stares at me. I fight against him to try to cover myself. Unintelligible pleas escape my throat as Tristan bats my hands away with the knife. He tightens his grip around my neck.

"The prize, Ashe, is ultimate freedom. Power. Enough money to never have to worry about the rat race. You will never worry about going hungry. You will never have to work a nine-to-five job. You can literally do whatever your soul desires. All you need to offer in return is a dedication and unwavering loyalty."

My breath hitches, "Loyalty to who?"

Tristan's black eyes stare directly into mine. "Loyalty to The Order."

"Are you sure this isn't some fucked up *Star Wars* cosplay? This sounds oddly familiar," I quip at him in an attempt to break his concentration.

For a split second, I can see something falter in Tristan's expression. His hold on me doesn't loosen.

Methodically, Tristan moves the knife to my collar bone. He traces the bone protruding just beneath the skin. Goosebumps appear in the spot he teased. The asshole smirks.

"I was planning on making this quick, but if you want to play, Ashe. Then let's play."

"I don't want shit to do with you," I spit at him.

Tristan chuckled. "Oh, but you do. Just look at how excited you are right now. Your nipples are begging to be teased."

He drags the tip of the blade from my collarbone down to the peak of my right breast. He circles my nipple with the blade, teasing it. My body stiffens before bending into his touch. Teeth grind together as my jaw locks into place, panic seizing my vocal cords. I know I should scream right now. Everything inside me is on high alert. Yet, I oddly feel the burn deep inside, that tingle when someone's touch felt just right.

"Ashe, the resident creepy girl. Tell me, darling, are you just as freaky in the dark as you are in the light?"

"Fuck. You," I bite out. My jaw begins to quiver under the pressure of my teeth grinding together.

"With pleasure. And then I'm going to gut you like the pig that you are." Tristan throws me to the ground. I land on my stomach and I can feel the broken rib shift inside. The knife clatters a few inches away.

"Come on, Ashe. It's time to die." Tristan mounts me, pinning my legs between his.

I scream. I can't tell if it is out loud or in my head, but I scream so hard I see stars.

No. Oh, god, please no. TRISTAN. Help!

"Yes, darling. Scream my name. That shit makes me so hard."

I squirm under his weight, trying to throw him off. Strong hands grab my hips and yank my ass in the air. One hand snakes around my side and pins my head to the damp earth. I'm bent over on the ground, gasping for air between screaming. Dirt begins to coat my chin, saliva mixing with the ground beneath my face. Tristan shifts forward and his hardened length presses against my center. I hear the faint sound of a zipper opening. Without warning, Tristan yanks my jeans down, exposing my bareness. My arms reach out, searching for the knife as calluses fingers trace my lower back.

"Tristan, stop," I beg him, but I don't even know if I believe myself at this point. It's all so confusing. My mind is swimming with adrenaline. I'm afraid. I'm turned on. At this moment, though, I know I will do almost anything to survive.

Tristan's finger dips lower, teasing my exposed heat. I'm regrettably wet and shamefully, waiting to see what he does next. My primal side is loving the thrill while my rational mind rages at me to fight. My hands still search the ground around me for the knife.

"You say stop, but look how wet you are for me, darling. Such a good little whore," he groans as he slips two fingers inside of me. I yelp at the intrusion and buck back at him in a futile attempt to remove his fingers. The movement only pushes him further. Despite being wet, I can feel the drag of his fingernails against my insides. Everything tightens at the unwanted attention. Searing heat radiates within me, microtears forming at each careless thrust of his fingers. Tristan grabs my hip with his other hand, locking me in place.

"You get off on being dominated, don't you? You fucking freak."

Tristan removes his fingers, leaving me empty. He brings his palm down on my ass. A cracking sound reverberates through the eerie silence. The assaulted cheek burns hot under his touch. He adjusts himself behind me, momentarily loosening his grip. His hand returns to rest on my lower back. A hardened tip presses against my exposed entrance. By some miracle, the tips of my fingers make contact with something cold and hard.

The knife...

Writhing against the human cage above me, I manage a few inches closer. Feeling the silky wood finally between my grip, I close my hand around the handle. In a last minute attempt to distract Tristan, I push myself up like

I'm ready to take him inside me. A mew of fake appreciation escapes my lips to lower his guard.

"That's right, darling. Let me fuck you into the afterlife." I could feel his hips move back, fingers grasping my folds open, ready to sink inside.

At the same time, I rolled over, knife in hand. I slash the knife directly at his face, making contact with his left eye. Tristan screams and falls backwards, reaching up to cover his serrated eyeball.

"You stupid cunt!" he spits at me, blood gushing between his fingers.

Anger flashed across his face. I scramble to my feet to steady myself. The knife is set in front of me, ready to attack again.

Tristan lunges toward me. I dodge him and stab him in the neck, the squelch of split skin making me queasy. It takes every ounce of strength to push down my gag reflex and stay on guard. He falters to the ground, both hands at his throat in a futile attempt to stop the bleeding. I crawl on top of him, centering myself on his now flaccid cock.

Tristan looks up at me, anger replaced by instinctual fear.

I stare down at him. Something in me shifts, hatred flows through my veins. Somewhere deep inside, I can feel this moment changing me. A demon grows from the depths of this depravity. Laughter bubbles up from inside and I cackle like an evil witch. I grabbed the knife with both hands and raise it over my head.

"Tell your little cult they can suck my metaphorical dick, Tristan."

I surge the knife down, square into his chest. Tristan screams as the knife plunges into his chest like butter. The screeching of bone against the blade is barely audible over

Tristan's wails. Blood sprays in all directions. I'm speckled head to toe as I raise my hands and drop them again. The sound of ripped tendon and cracked bone is the symphony of my descent into madness. I continue stabbing him with every ounce of hatred until I'm left panting, no longer able to raise my arms.

A cavity the size of a golf ball stares up at me. Blood, flesh, and bone shards mix in the center. Tristan's lifeless eyes stare back at me. His skin pales with each passing second. Yanking the knife from his rib cage, I wipe the blood on my tattered clothes. I shove myself off of the lifeless body and stare in disbelief.

Holy. Shit.

I did it.

I just killed someone.

I tie my shredded shirt into a crude bra and pull my pants up where they belong. On instinct, I start grabbing my belongings from the area. I shove the knife into my bag and pick up all the pieces of torn clothing, just like I learned in all those hours binging murder podcasts.

Walking in a circle, I scan the area for any place to drag Tristan's lifeless body. I need him to be hidden for at least six months; enough time for decomposition to kick in and remove any organic traces of evidence. I can't go to the police. They would never believe me.

It didn't take long to find what I needed. Near the northwest corner was a ravine down to the river that filtered into the lake.

Perfect.

It takes all of my energy and a lot of breaks, but I drag the corpse to the edge of the cliff. With one final shove, the body descends down the rocky side. Faint clicks of bone on rock wafts through the night. After a few moments, the sound of a splash ripples from the river below. The shadow of a body is barely visible in its resting spot. The water eagerly welcomes its new friend into the murky depths.

"Rest in pieces, asshole." Unceremoniously, I walk back to grab my bag and hike back to my car.

PRESENT

After that night, I vowed to never tell anyone what happened. I was lucky enough the cuts Tristan gave me on my face healed quickly, barely a scar left behind. They only appear under black light, which I avoid like the plague. I don't need anyone asking questions they certainly don't want the answer to. I wouldn't even know how to answer them. I repeat that night over and over again in my mind, searching for some redeeming quality in my actions.

Eventually, the body was found and everyone assumed it was The Senior Slayer. The corpse was so decomposed from rotting in the chilled depths of the lake, no one questioned it. Nothing was traced back to me. I couldn't reveal my secret because, despite what I wanted, I liked it. Not only the roughness, but the excitement of the knife against my skin. The fear of whether or not I would survive. The crunch beneath my hands as I carved into the body. The slickness of the blood sliding over my skin. A warm blanket of grotesque desire. That night awoke something that was sleeping deep inside. Something I thought I had avoided growing up. The quiet, creepy girl transformed into a dark goddess of power. Every sexual encounter from then on was an experiment.

How far could I push my dark desires before going over the edge into oblivion?

The only disturbing remembrance of that encounter happened on graduation day. A small letter was tucked away in my diploma.

CONGRATULATIONS ON WINNING THE GAME. WELCOME TO THE ORDER, MS. NIKKO.

Attached to the letter was a check for over $2.5 Million from *The Order, Inc.*

I stared in disbelief before ripping the letter to shreds. I looked around at the other graduates. Everyone was smiling and happy, celebrating their success and survival of senior year. No one was noticing the panic attack I was having internally. I scanned the crowd and stopped on a figure at the far corner of the bleachers. Under the last row in the shadows stood a man with a skull mask.

The skull mask.

All the blood left my body. We locked eyes. Minutes passed by as the world disappeared around me. A ringing in my ears drowned out the celebration.

Suddenly, the figure shook its head at me before disappearing behind the bleachers. I break out in a full sprint, weaving in and out of people embracing their loved ones and friends sharing a secret celebratory drink with the flask they snuck in.

By the time I made it to the edge of the bleachers, the stranger was gone.

KNOCK, KNOCK, KNOCK.

TIME TO DIE

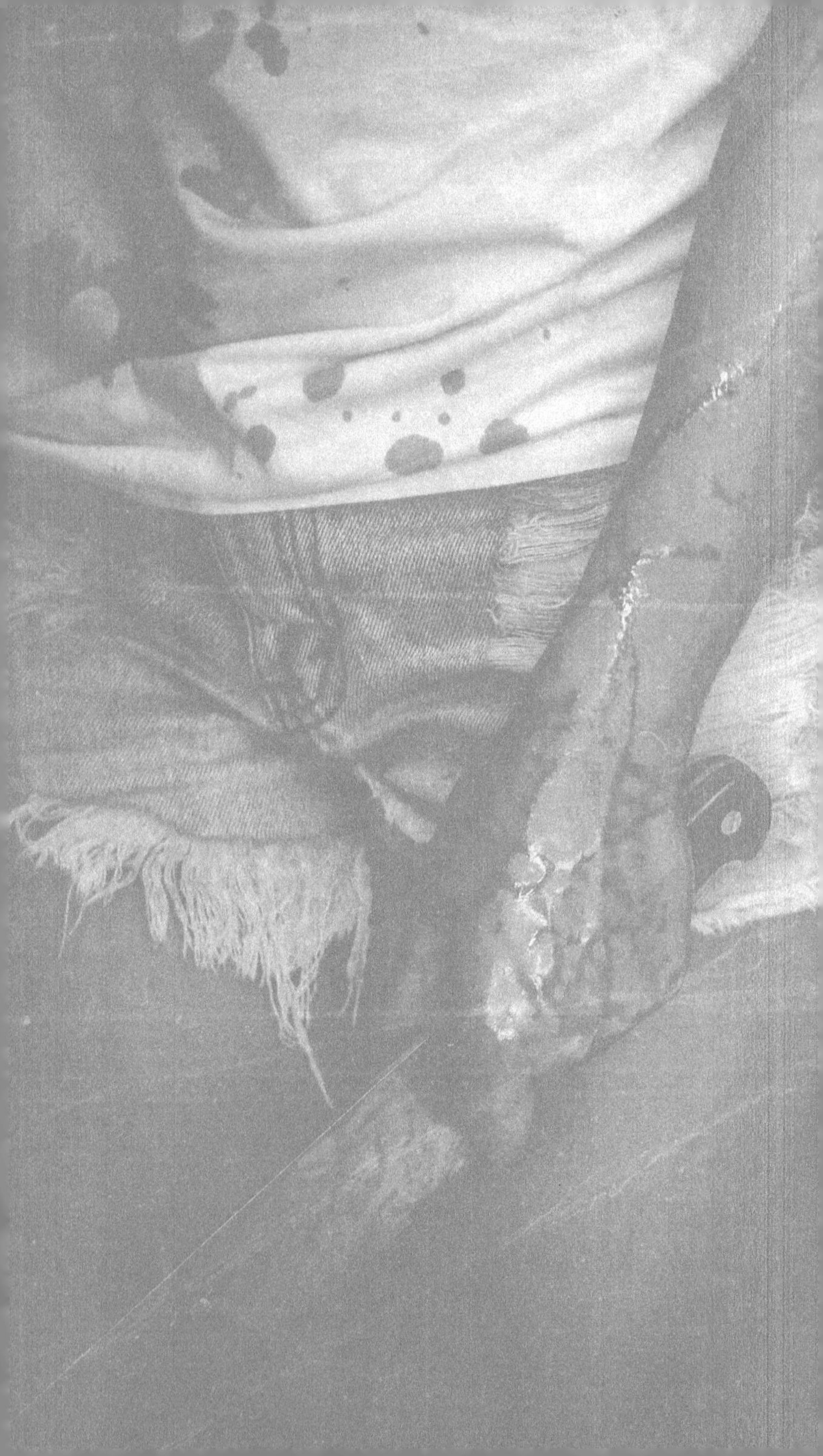

SIX

I'm jolted from reliving my nightmare by a pounding coming from the front door. Everyone freezes, staring in the direction of the strange noise. There's no mistaking the loud knock we hear coming from the other side. Each one of us is waiting to see what the other will do.

Another set of knocks rings through the cabin. This time less forceful. A powerful voice calls through the wooden protector between us and the outside intruder.

"County Sheriffs. We're here to speak with the cabin owner, Mr. James."

Sam cries out like she's in agony and pulls herself deeper into her blanket. Jason flinches in his seat, but doesn't move his eyes away from me. The questionable look remains on his face. Colton sighs before pushing up to his feet. I sit frozen in place. My eyes follow him to the door.

Colton shuffles slowly to the entryway. His shoulders

slumped like the whole weight of the world is on his shoulders. His tanned hand reaches out to grasp the copper handle. With one swift swing, the door opens to reveal two uniformed men standing on the front porch. I don't recognize either of them, which is surprising because I know the entire department thanks to my research on The Slayer.

The one in front, who I presume knocked on the door, is tall and slender. His high and tight is hidden underneath the uniform hat atop his head. From where I sit, blue eyes crinkle at the corners and his face is set in a permanent grimace. He stands with authority and makes direct eye contact with Colton. A no-nonsense deputy who's probably seen his fair share of bullshit. The man behind him is shorter in stature and stocky. His body strains behind his uniform. The outline of defined muscle clearly marked. Noticeably younger, too. If I had to guess, he wrestled in his lifetime and now spends his off time lifting heavy things in the gym. His smooth shaven face gives away his age. His brown eyes are bright with curiosity and naivety. Clearly, he hasn't seen anything yet to sour his love of the job.

The three speak for a moment. Their conversation is too low for any of us to hear them. The younger deputy stares over Colton's shoulder at the three of us still sitting. His eyes linger just long enough that I know exactly what he's doing. He's assessing the room and making mental notes of all of us. Who could be a suspect? Who would be stupid enough to pull off this prank? Do any of us look inebriated enough to be making up the whole thing? A myriad of plausible motives to work through in a matter of seconds.

Deputy Muscles makes eye contact with me. I'm staring right back, trying to figure out if they can even be trusted. From the research for my books and the countless hours of being interrogated when I first started writing, I know first hand that the police work in this town is subpar, at best. A small town department overwhelmed by big city crime after The Slayer showed his gruesome tricks. The amount of missed evidence or poorly secured crime scenes have been astounding. The general public was so engrossed in fear that they overlooked the department's mishaps. Plus, I know first hand that the killer keeps tabs on the town. Who's to say he hasn't infiltrated the police force or paid them off like some slasher hungry mobster?

I offer Deputy Muscles a tight smile to show that I'm not the one to be worried about. His face noticeably shifts. He's no longer looking at me with suspicion. I watch as his eyes widen and the look of recognition crosses his face.

Son of a bitch.

He recognizes me.

Perfect.

Great.

Exactly what we fucking need right now.

Colton waves the men inside and follows quickly behind them as they make their way to the living room where we all sit. Deputy Serious nods up and down as he acknowledges all of us. His rookie behind him giddy with excitement.

"Good afternoon, kids. My name is Deputy Harden. This here is my partner, Deputy Ramirez. We're here because one of you reported evidence of The Senior Slayer in the area."

Colton makes introductions for us. "Yes, sir. This is Jason, Sam, and Ashe."

Sam peeks up from her blanket long enough to give a small wave. She's no longer crying and listening very intently to every word that comes out of the Deputy's mouth. Her green eyes are dimmed more than usual. Jason sends a welcoming nod to the Deputy. His body language says he's still tense, but he's hiding it pretty well. When they get to me, I try to give my most endearing smile possible with a little wave. Anything to not give my usual resting bitch face and paint an unnecessary target on my back.

Deputy Ramirez speaks up, "I'm sorry. I have to ask. Are you *the Ashe*. Like Ashe Nikko, author of the goremance novels that's been all over TikTok? Your work is amazing!"

Deputy Harden shoots a deadened glare at his rookie who's currently fan-girling over me.

"Horror Romance, but guilty. Thank you for the kind words, Deputy," I say, shyly. I'll never get used to being recognized by strangers.

Deputy Harden pinches the bridge of his nose, scrunching his eyes with a sigh.

"Ramirez, can you act professional for five damn seconds, please?"

Deputy Ramirez squares his shoulders and stands up straight.

"Yes, sir. Sorry, sir."

"And stop calling me sir! I'm your partner, not your Drill Sergeant." Harden huffs.

I slap a hand over my mouth to stifle a laugh. These are the most animated cops I've ever seen. I don't recall meeting either of them in the past, which means they might actually take us seriously. It makes the whole situation a little more bearable.

Harden collects himself before continuing.

"As I was saying, we want all the information you kids can give. Anything that you think might be important."

Jason jolts up without warning. He walks over to the

table and picks up the mask to hand to the deputies. He's all serious, no hint of the joker Jason we all know.

"Sam found this down in the lake shed. We all talked; none of us planted it there. We don't think this is some prank. If you look at the carving in the forehead, it looks and *smells* like real blood. We don't know anyone who would try to do this."

Harden takes the mask from Jason. He flips it over in his hands as he analyzes it. After a minute, he hands it to Ramirez. Ramirez is all serious now as he examines the mask in his hands. The two deputies glance at each other for a second. A knowing look is shared between them.

"Can you excuse us for a second?" Harden dismisses them as they walk towards the front door.

We all sit in the living room staring after them.

Sam mumbles from her spot on the couch, "What the hell does that mean?"

Five minutes pass before the pair return. Their expressions have noticeably changed. Both are serious and straight faced. Harden takes charge again.

"We're going to take this for safe keeping, but rest assured there's nothing to worry about. There's no copy cat on the loose. The killer hasn't returned."

"How can you be so sure?" Sam squeaks out.

"We have a dedicated team for this stuff. Trust us. You have nothing to worry about," Ramirez adds.

I scoff. We should've expected nothing less from them. Of course, they're not going to take this seriously.

"But what about the blood?" I push.

Harden raises his hand. "That's of no concern. For all we know it's just fake blood from the local prop store. We can analyze it back at the department, if you like."

"Yes, actually. I fucking would, if you don't mind," I bite back.

Harden narrows his stare at me. I look back at him, not backing down. I'm not taking their dismissal for an answer. That mask is seared into my memory. I know it better than I know my own face. I know it's real.

After a beat, Ramirez pipes in, "If you guys find anything else, you can call us directly. We can come back out at any time." He hands Colton his business card. Colton nods and takes the card, placing it in his back pocket.

The deputies nod goodbye and make their exit. We're left with even more questions than before they arrived. When the door snaps closed, we're met again with the growing realization of our deepest fears.

TIME TO DIE

SEVEN

I stand under the water of the shower feeling the hot beads fall over my skin. The shower head sings above me as steam fills the tiny guest bathroom. I sigh into the cascading water, a momentary mental break from reality.

The sheriffs didn't provide us with any piece of mind. They dismissed our allegations that the killer could be here. On top of that, they treated us like ignorant children. Little do they know, at least one of us has been through enough shit in their lifetime to know when we're being lied to.

Neither of the guys were happy that the cops left with the mask. Colton mumbled something under his breath about hiding evidence after he closed the door before heading to the kitchen. Bottles jingled from the doorway, which could only mean Colton was ready for another stiff drink. Jason got up in a huff and stalked off. He didn't say a word to anyone on his way out. It felt odd that he wasn't making some childish joke or trying to undress me with his eyes. Honestly, it was straight up unnerving to see him so out of character. He's been holed up in his room ever since.

Sam asked if I could stay with her in the living room. We sat together on the couch under her blanket as I listened to all the happy memories she had of our summer vacations. Her laughter filled the tense air as she recounted our last trip when Colton ripped his trunks trying to back flip off the dock. I could tell she was trying to change the vibe in the cabin from negative doom and gloom to something more joyful.

We stayed like that for almost an hour before I decided it was time to have some alone time. I love reminiscing with Sam and being in her energy, but I had too much pent up anxiety to sit there any longer. I needed a shower or an orgasm. I didn't care which one came first. It wouldn't be the first time I took care of myself on one of our little trips. However, after ten minutes of laying on my bed circling my clit with my pocket vibrator, I gave up. Nothing I did was bringing me to the edge. Frustrated, I threw the toy back in my bag and grabbed my towel before heading to the bathroom.

Now the burning water left my skin numb and deadened my frazzled nerves. Still, it didn't sate me. The pulsing ache I felt between my legs reminded me that I was stuck here without relief until our trip ended. I trail my hand down between my thighs in an attempt to feel something. I groan into the space, frustrated that I was so close and couldn't get myself off. I mentally curse myself for not scheduling a play session with someone on my roster prior to this trip. It had been a few weeks since my last session, but I assumed this trip would be a stress free break from reality.

What a great fucking joke the universe gave me.

Accepting the fact I wasn't getting anywhere, I turn off the water. I step out of the shower with my towel wrapped around my damp body. I check my phone to see if there's any missed messages. It's somehow already 7:15 p.m. My stomach growls in protest, reminding me that, yes, it's getting late. We still haven't eaten yet since we left home this morning, skipping lunch thanks to our grim discovery.

I catch a glimpse of myself in the steamed mirror. Haunted eyes stare back from a pale face. Blue hair pulled into a messy bun. Water droplets covering the art on my arms cast a sparkle over each tattoo like galactic glitter. Beaded liquid clings to my exposed ink that sits across my breasts, just above where I tucked the towel into my armpit. The lush fabric barely covers my curves. Toned legs extended below the hem of the fabric as the towel drapes over the roundness of my behind. The intersection where the two ends of the towel meet leaves a sliver of a shadow concealing the dip where my legs meet my hips.

I sigh at my reflection.

Think happy thoughts. Everything is going to be fine. You're just overthinking things.

I take a few deep breaths before turning to leave the bathroom.

The hallway is eerily quiet as I sneak my way to my bedroom. Glancing down to the end, Jason's door is still closed. I really hope his sour mood won't last all weekend. I was actually enjoying this new side of him. I never pegged him to be the dominant type. I'll never admit it out loud, but I'm willing to test that theory should the opportunity arise.

As I reach my door, I notice it's not closed like I left it. A small glimmer of light escapes from the edge of the door.

Sam must've came in to borrow one of my hoodies. I push the door fully open. Nothing seems too out of place as I glance around. My duffle bag in the corner is open with a pile of clothes. I dump my phone in the end table before walking over to inspect it. As suspected, a hoodie is missing.

I dig through the bag searching for my sleep shirt and flowy shorts. Finding what I want, I turn to place everything on the bed to change. I stop short. Fear strikes through me.

On the bed is a note that definitely wasn't there when I left to take a shower. Afraid to move, I scan the room again. Not seeing anything else out of place, I hesitantly reach out to pick it up.

Written on a yellowed notepad paper in large red letters, it reads:

"ARE YOU READY TO PLAY, ASHE?"

Before I can register what's happening, strong hands are on me. One arm wraps around my waist, pulling me into a toned body. The other covers my face, muffling my cry for help. Panic rises inside of me filling every nerve. I struggle against the unwelcome intruder, kicking in the air. My arms claw at the hand over my mouth trying to break free. The intruder's grip tightens. I can feel as they lean in. Their warm breath on the back of my neck. I still. We stand there for a beat in silence.

Low and demanding, the intruder breaks the silence.

"I told you I would fill that smart mouth. What is the safe word?"

Chills radiate over my body. I wiggle my mouth free just enough to cuss back, "Jason?! What the fuck? Let me go!"

Jason chuckles and readjusts his grip on me.

"I didn't fucking stutter, Ashe. Either tell me no or answer the question. Safe word. Now."

He removes his hand a fraction to allow me to answer. I contemplate shoving him off, but something inside me hums at the excitement. My body wants to play. The tension in the air is heady.

"Eat a dick, Jason," I mumble, ignoring my growing desire.

Jason loosens his grip. I try to run, making it a few feet in front of him towards the door, but I'm not fast enough. He grabs my wrist and yanks me back. I yelp at his touch. Spinning me around, Jason pulls me close. His left hand snakes around my waist with his right hand now brandishing a knife. It sets gently to my throat. I can feel every inch of him pushed up against me through my damp towel. His biceps strain against the black t-shirt he's wearing. His jeans are flush over his toned leg he placed between my own. The fabric rubs gently over my clit. His growing erection presses against my stomach. My breath hitches.

"I'm going to ask nicely one more time. What. Is. The. Safe. Word?"

I look up at him. Dark eyes stare back clouded with want. I hold his gaze, challenging him further. I watch a feather of a smile dance across his chiseled features. My insides melt under his gaze. I'm entranced by this powerful energy I've never seen from him before. He digs the blade into my neck waiting for an answer. The sharp edge bites into my skin and I wince at the pain.

I take a ragged breath, giving into the darkness lurking under the surface.

"Slayer," I rasp out.

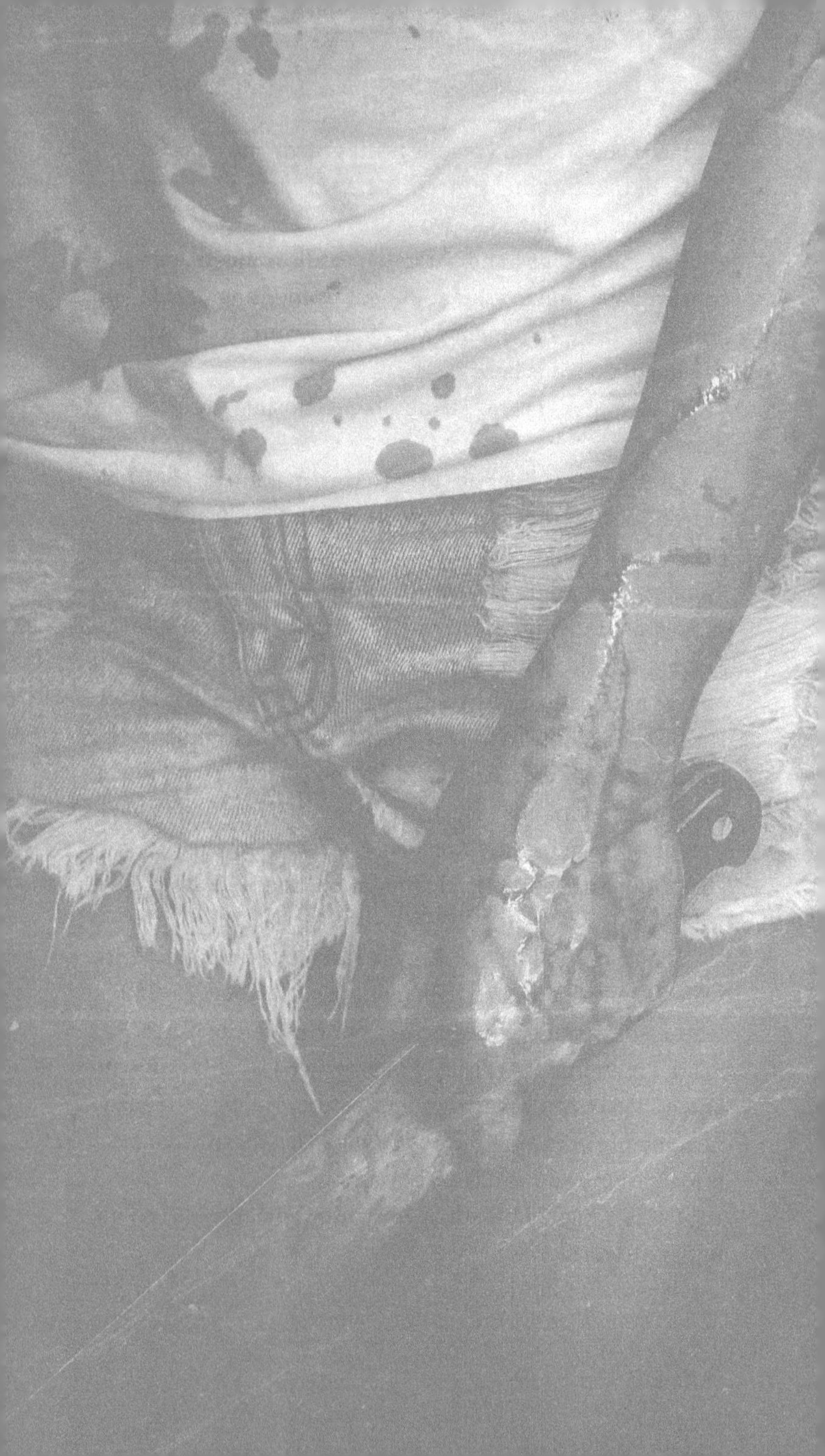

EIGHT

Alow growl escapes deep inside of Jason. He smirks at my submission.

With a death grip on my neck, he throws me against the wall behind me. My back slams into the cold surface, knocking the air from my lungs. I gasp at the contact; so familiar yet, this time, more intimate. The blade still at my neck, Jason's lips crash down on mine. They're soft in contrast to the roughness he's taking me. He nips at my lower lip, making me gasp before invading my mouth with his tongue. My hands find their way under his shirt. I dig my nails into his chest, receiving an appreciative groan from him.

We stand there devouring each other for what feels like forever. I had always dreamed what kissing him would feel like. Rum mixed with pineapple brings up the memory of our almost kiss that fateful night. Still covered in the towel,

I lean my wet body into him to deepen the kiss. If I'm going down the rabbit hole, I'm going all in.

Jason grabs the towel with his other hand, launching it across the room and leaves me fully exposed. He breaks the kiss to look down at me. I'm left panting, my head is spinning with excitement. Jason's eyes darken as he takes me in. My body sings under his appreciative gaze. His free hand finds its way to my breast, teasing the sensitive skin while his thumb brushes gently over my budding nipple. Instinctually, I lean into his touch. A mew of appreciation escapes my lips as my breathing picks up. I lull my head back against the wall, savoring each swipe of his thumb. Jason leans and nips at the pulsating artery in my neck.

"Fuck," I rasp out.

Jason chuckles into my neck as he continues his assault.

"You think you can fool Sam. Colton. The officers. But I know the secret you're hiding, Ashe," he taunts.

My eyes flash open. He's leaning back to look at me, staring directly into my soul. I can feel ice forming around my blackened heart.

No. There's no way. No one knows. No one, except...except the killer.

Bile rises in my throat. Horniness be damned, my flight or fight kicks in. I can't believe I didn't see it sooner. Fucking idiot.

I reposition myself against the wall ready to run. I try pushing Jason's chest to get him away from me. He doesn't budge.

"Get away from me, Jason. You know nothing about my secrets." I push again.

A chuckle escapes from his lips, the corners of his mouth upturned. I can feel his grip on the knife tighten.

"Oh, but that's where you're wrong, little bat. You put

on this facade of the dark, mysterious, dominating goth queen. I know what you truly are. What you truly want."

"And what is that, oh wise one?" I snip at him.

Jason removes the knife from my neck. The metallic tip traces its way down my neck and across my tits. He flicks the tip of the knife at the top of my sternum, effectively nicking me. I suppress the scream rising inside me and continue staring directly at Jason. Warm, crimson droplets run down my stomach. Blood begins to bead at the cut and Jason holds the knife in place, gathering a pool of blood against the reflective surface.

Jason brings the blade up to his mouth, examining the dark liquid that clings to the metal. In one swift movement, his tongue meets the blunt edge and he licks one side clean. He sighs.

"Fucking delicious, just like I thought you would be. I can't wait to see what your pussy tastes like."

He brings the knife in front of my mouth, turning it so the tip is poised delicately against my Cupid's bow.

"What you want is to be dominated. That bratty exterior is only a cover. You're just waiting for someone to match your energy," he says. The knife drops to my bottom lip, playing against the soft skin.

I'm panting again, but this time in fear of being sliced like Black Dahlia. My brain is screaming at me: *Run. Run now. Runnnnn.*

I'm immovable, in shock for what just happened. For what Jason just said.

He pushes the tip of the knife further onto my bottom lip. "Open your mouth," Jason chides.

I look down at the knife and back at Jason.

"No," I say.

Jason shakes his head.

"That wasn't a request, little bat. *Open.*"

He gestures with the knife.

I lick my lips, still panting. I contemplate whether or not I trust him enough to not dice me up.

Against my better judgment, I part my mouth just enough for the tip to slip inside.

"Good girl. Now close," Jason says.

I do as I'm told. Partly because I don't want to die. Partly because this is kind of fucking hot. My lips close around the bloodied tip. The salty tinge is familiar against my tongue.

Jason is smirking again.

"Suck," he whispers.

I hold back a whimper and follow his instructions. Carefully, I suck. Using my tongue on the blunt side, I lick at the remaining blood like I'm giving the blowjob of a lifetime. Jason readjusts himself as he admires my handiwork.

We stand there in silence. The sound of my tongue lapping up the metallic, sticky juices filling the space. Jason doesn't take his eyes off mine. Those dark, amber pools bore deeper into mine, uncovering years worth of pent up disappointment. I'm completely disarmed, lost in their depths. My past, present, and future all lie at his hands. I stare back, taking every drop of blood off the blade, this unholy act marking the change of our friendship forever.

When the blade has no more left to give, Jason removes it from my mouth. He reaches behind him and produces the sheath for the blade. Not breaking eye contact, he slips the silver tip back into its carrier. His hand reaches down between my legs. He places the hilt of the knife firmly against my swollen clit as he holds the sheathed blade. I flinch at the touch of something so foreign. I love knife play, but I have never dared put it there during play time.

"You're doing such a good job. I knew you could follow directions like the good girl you are. My little bat deserves a prize," he coos. The leather presses harder against my arousal. "Ride this knife like your life depends on it."

His lips cover mine again, distracting me before I could think about what we're doing. He parts my mouth with his tongue, not asking for entrance as he takes me. The taste of rum and pineapple mixes with iron. A heady concoction that makes me moan in appreciation.

Jason groans in response. "That's it, baby. Just imagine what it'll feel like with my cock between those juicy thighs."

Gently, I roll my hips forward towards his hand and back against the wall. The smooth leather glides against my clit. The softness is so similar to skin; I imagine it's Jason's cock between my thighs. The finger grips dig at my pelvis, increasing the sensations. I pick up the pace, accepting my fate. I ride the hilt wishing it was his cock there, teasing my sensitive clit. He holds the knife steady as I continue to grind my way to ecstasy. I gasp into his mouth as my high finds me.

"Oh, fuck. I'm so close. Oh my god, Jason!"

Waves of ecstasy ripple through me. The release I so desperately searched for before my shower hits me. I'm gasping against his lips as my body lets go of every ounce of stress that I had leading up to this weekend. My legs tremble at the climax.

Jason leans back to look at me. His gaze sated, yet demanding. "Look at how beautiful you are cumming at my command. I knew you could be a good little slut for me."

Jason plants a gentle kiss to my forehead and removes the knife from between my thighs, placing it in his back pocket. He steps back far enough for me to stand straight.

He keeps a hand on my waist to steady me as I come down from my high. His expression, once shrouded in desire, is softer. His eyes return to their golden amber hue. He runs a hand through his hair, fixing it back into place.

"Well. That was...unexpected," he chuckles.

My face warms at the comment.

Am I blushing?!

I look over at the door that's still closed. We can hear faint banging of cabinets coming from the other side. Muffled voices seep in from under the door.

Looking back at Jason, he's smirking. Again.

Asshole.

"If you breathe a *word*–," I start.

Jason rolls his eyes at me as he begins towards the door.

"Please, Ashe. Don't flatter yourself," he says flippantly, pulling the door open.

"I'm serious, Jason. Not a damn word," I bark at him. I'm seething. The high of my release dissipated as quickly as it came. Common sense has, indeed, returned. If the others knew what just happened it would cause the most awkward conversation in existence. It wasn't my plan to make our friendship messy.

Jason turns to look at me as he passes through the door.

"You think I'm done with you?" He chuckles. "That's cute. Now be a good little bat and get dressed. We have dinner to make."

He winks at me before disappearing out of the room.

"God damn it, Jason. You're such an asshole!" I yell after him. I walk over to the door, slamming it for dramatic effect. I can hear him laughing down the hall.

I turn to lean against the door. The weight of what just happens washes over me. Leaning my head back against the door, I take a few deep breaths trying to clear my mind.

I assumed we'd get in bed one day. I just didn't assume it would be this weekend. I didn't assume it would be so dark...and unforgivably hot.

The smell of burgers waft into the space. A reminder that the weekend is still young and this day isn't even over yet.

With a final deep breath, I push off the door and return to my bag. Searching for my baggiest t-shirt and shorts, I get dressed. Racking a comb through my disheveled, damp hair, I pull it back into a loose bun. I roll my neck left and right in a useless attempt to release some tension.

Jason thinks he can push me around this weekend. He *thinks* he can force me into pure submission.

HA.

He wishes.

I have my own games to play and they have only just begun.

"Well, then," I mumble to myself. "Game on, Jason. Game fucking on."

NINE

The delicious aroma of burgers cooking on a charcoal grill is undeniable as I finish up in my room. I check my phone before plugging it into the charger. It's almost 8:00 p.m. Late dinner is always a custom during our weekend getaways. There's no better feeling than winding down with the sunset while Colton cooks his famous burgers. Sam usually whips up her fancy herbal cocktails that she swears gives her the best night's sleep. Jason is always up to his usual antics, providing the comedic relief. We can sit outside for hours reminiscing about the good times until the stars come out. It's the thing I cherish the most about these trips.

I finish getting dressed after my very impromptu foreplay session. The note Jason wrote me before his unexpected appearance sits next to my phone on the nightstand. Red ink teases me as a reminder of other memories that could be made this weekend. I close my eyes, counting my breathing again.

One, two, three; out.

Two, two, three; out.

Three, two, three; out.

I open them expecting to feel calmer. I don't. Annoyance simmers just under my skin. I can't forgive myself for allowing Jason to get to me so easily. Fuck that. Instead of denying the inevitable, I'm going to get on top of it. Well, on top of him.

I open my door and step into the hallway to head downstairs. The lights are off as I descend down the stairs, a gentle glow rises up from the first floor. I know not to linger for too long or the group will wonder where I'm at. Even worse, Jason might tell them what happened between us moments ago. The faint warmness of his body still lingers, the sweet tingle of release radiates from my core despite the growing irritation. I distinctly remember him saying he wouldn't tell. However, at this point, I can't predict what he'll do anymore.

As I pass the wall of sliding glass doors that lead to the deck, I spy Colton manning the grill. He's on the phone while he flips the patties absentmindedly. I can't make out who he's talking to, but his face is scrunched into a grimace. His muscles are tense under the gray t-shirt that sits taught against his body. It must be something serious to get Colton worked up during a vacation trip. I send a prayer to the universe hoping that it's nothing to do with his new football contract.

Laughter spills from the entryway to the kitchen. I grin. I know Sam's boisterous laugh better than anyone. It's reassuring to know the debacle with the mask didn't damper her spirits. Out of everyone, she's the most sensitive and I love her for it. Not that she needs protecting, she can hold her own. There were plenty of times growing up that Sam would end the fight that my loud mouth ultimately started. Sam might be small, but she is mighty. May the gods have mercy on anyone who crosses paths with her protecting the ones she loves.

My thoughts are cut short when I spot Jason leaning against the counter. My eyes linger too long over his muscular frame. He's changed into a pair of gray sweatpants and a baggy, black t-shirt. I find myself especially distracted by the way the sweatpants hug the best part of him. A not so subtle outline of his dick teases me from across the room. The sight of him goes straight to my midsection. I might as well go change because I'm dripping wet again.

Carnal need rises from deep inside. I push it down, locking it away in the time-out cage I envision in my mind.

I came down here ready for war. It appears Jason was two steps ahead of me.

Jason catches my ogling. His lips turn up into the most mischievous, shit-eating grin. As if on cue, he reaches his arms over his head to stretch. His shirt lifts enough for me to see the faint outline of a V at the hem of his pants.

I gasp. Audibly. Like an idiot. His eyes dart back to mine and raises his eyebrows in my direction.

He doesn't break his conversation with Sam. She's completely oblivious to this interaction or the fact that I'm here. When she turns around, she doesn't even mention the fact that Jason looks like the physical embodiment of every girl's book boyfriend.

"Oh, you're back! Dinner is almost ready. Colton is making burgers while Jason helps me prep the sides. Are you thirsty?"

I shrug my shoulders. If I'm going to make this cat and mouse game work in my favor, I need to act natural.

"I am, but I think I need something a little stronger before I have one of your infamous tinctures," I say, making my way around the island to the liquor cabinet. The frosted bottle of rum beckons to me. Another dark and stormy should do the trick.

I grunt as I reach to the top shelf for a copper mug.

Dark and stormy. How ironic that my favorite drink now describes my sex life.

"Ashe, I know you love your rum, but you should really have an elderberry spritzer instead if you want to avoid a hangover tomorrow," Sam chastises as I finish mixing my drink, careful to only do a half pour of the liquor. I can still drink and keep my wits about me.

I turn around with the copper mug in hand.

"Sam, I will do whatever detox you whip up for me after this trip. I promise. Right now, I really just need to clear my head."

Sam rolls her eyes at me before turning back to the salad she was preparing.

"Whatever, babes. Don't come crying to me when you feel like a dump truck ran you over. I wish you would try meditating with me instead of drinking. It's better for your soul."

"If I even have a soul," I mutter.

I lift the copper vessel up to take a sip, but it quickly disappears from my grasp. I look down at my empty hand in disbelief before tracking where the drink went.

Jason is standing next to me, mug in hand. He lifts it to his lips and chugs the contents down in one gulp.

"What the actual fuck, Jason! Make your own damn drink," I bark at him.

Sam glances up from her veggies, eyes cautious, before going back to cutting. If she's attempting to fake her minding her business, the smile on her face gives her away.

He places the mug down on the counter before leaning down to be eye level with my face.

"Sam said you shouldn't be drinking. I'm just trying to help." His voice is low, laced with temptation and a warning. The smell of lime and spices hangs in the air.

I look down at his mouth, wishing we were the only ones here so I could kiss him again. I lick my lips thinking of the interaction we had back in my room. Jason snorts before straightening himself. I swear I could hear him mumble, "Not the place, little bat."

"Thank you, Jason. Maybe next you could find your way to Ashe's room tonight and help her see Divine Intervention." Sam says smirking, pointing a knife between us.

I stare at her. Mouth gaped open. I *cannot* believe she just said that out loud.

Jason casually throws an arm over my shoulders.

"Are you playing matchmaker, Sam? That's so sweet of you," he says as he pulls me closer, his hand firm around my arm. I can feel his body heat even though there's a layer of clothing separating our bodies. I stiffen under his touch, waiting for this mortifying moment to be over.

"I would rather be tied up and tortured than find you in my room tonight, Jason," I say, feigning disinterest. I playfully jab my elbow into Jason's side to release his hold on me. He grunts, grabbing his side. I take the opportunity to spin myself out of his grasp. In three giant steps, I'm on the other side of the room to make some distance between us and hop up on the counter. Jason rights himself as I settle my ass on the cold marble. His hands rest behind him as he leans back again.

"Kinky," he quips. "If I didn't know any better, I would say that you've already fantasized me with my clothes off." He winks at me with that stupid ass grin on his face. He's choosing to play dumb. Like me.

"I assumed you tried propositioning her earlier from the yelling I heard up stairs," Sam giggles as she turns around to grab more dishes from the cabinet behind her.

"No. Jason thinks it's funny to leave threatening notes in people's rooms."

I raise my hand to give him my favorite finger. He snickers and I shoot him the death glare. My peripherals catch a ripple under his shirt. His body is rigid even though his laughter seems care-free. My gaze follows down his arm to where his hands rest. White knuckles grip around the edge of the counter top.

I suck in a breath. My eyes dart back to his.

The grin remains on his face, but it's a ruse. His eyes bore into mine. I can't pin the expression he's trying to hide. Dark, swirling pools of something sinister lurks underneath that amber gaze. Butterflies flutter in my stomach, anticipation and curiosity of what he could do to me.

"I think you smoked too much with Sam earlier. I didn't leave a note in your room, Ashe." His tone is clipped.

I glare at him in disbelief. Is he really playing *that* stupid?

"Yes, you did. It had red ink and it said, *time to play.* That's your M.O."

He snorts, rolling his eyes and turns to Sam, "Did you give her 'shrooms again?"

"Nope. None this trip. I only brought my trusty friend, Mary Jane, this time," Sam says as she continues digging through the cabinet.

I throw my hands in the air. "Are you in on this, too?"

Sam shakes her head, still buried in her search.

I turn my attention back to Jason, pointing a finger at him. "Stop fucking with me. I know it was you. You're the only one twisted like me to play a prank like that."

Jason stands up and crosses his arms across his chest.

Defensive move, Jason. I see that.

"I can assure you, Ashe. As much as I love seeing you get wound up, whatever note you're going on about wasn't from me. However, I will be storing that away for a later date." Amusement flits across his chiseled features.

I hop off the counter, marching over to him. I look up at him with all the anger I can muster.

"So you're telling me some stranger just wandered into my room to place a cryptic note and it wasn't you? The one who's been trying to get with me since this morning. The one who..."

I clamp my mouth shut before I reveal too much, teeth clattering together. I step back from him, still fuming.

"The one what, Ashe?" Jason asks smugly, cocking his head to one side. He leans into me, but says nothing. His stare goads me to keep going.

All I see is red, fiery anger. He knew exactly how this conversation would go. He knew I would be backed into a corner and be tempted to give away our secret in a fit of exasperation. If I could claw his face off right now like a wildebeest, I would.

"You know what? Fine. Fine, Jason. It wasn't you. The Gods' gift to Earth is innocent. Then who the hell left the note in my room?" I question.

A loud bang comes from behind us. We jump apart and stare towards the glass doors. Colton comes into the frame of the kitchen doorway.

"Alright, kids. Stop fighting. You can flirt later once

everyone is ready for bed." Colton sets down a plate of burgers on the island.

I glare at him. "We weren't flirting. He's being an ass."

Colton laughs. Full-on belly laughs in my face.

"Ashe, I already know. We're all aware of whatever is going on between you two. All I ask, as your friend, is that you remember our friendship comes first."

I freeze. Everything inside me goes numb.

He doesn't trust me.

I clench my jaw shut again as tears well behind my eyes. I stare at my friends like I'm a stranger to them. Despite all the years together, this is how they view me?

While the idea of hooking up with Jason isn't the worst decision I could make in this lifetime, it definitely wasn't the one I premeditated to make on this trip. The fact that Colton even questions my decision making in jeopardizing the group instead of Jason's insistent nagging is disheartening.

Why am I the one being interrogated when Jason was the one who started this?

"Wow, Colton. That's low. Real low. I'm over here saying he's the one starting all of this and you're accusing me as the instigator?" Now I'm the one crossing my arms, pouting.

"While I agree that Jason can be an ass sometimes, he didn't leave the note. He came down to help me start the grill while you were in the shower and then went to his room for a work call. He's got an alibi," Colton says, grabbing a plate from the counter. He wanders over to the fixings to make his dinner.

I stare at him.

"Are you so sure about that? He was in my room after I got out of the shower."

Colton pauses mid-grab of a burger patty and looks up at me. A slight slip of a grin crosses his face.

"Was he now? Well then, looks like you're on your own, bro." He shrugs as he continues adding food to his plate.

I turn back to Jason, stomping my feet like a juvenile child having a melt down.

"See?! It was you."

He holds his arms up. "Ashe, I swear to god. It wasn't from me."

"Screw the note. I have a better question. Why were you up in her room, Jay?" Colton mumbles with his mouth full. His eyes light up with the prospect of gossip.

Jason looks down to me, a Cheshire grin painted across his beautiful, mesmerizing face. He takes a deep breath before looking back up at Colton.

"Well, if you must know. Ashe and I..."

"Guys," Sam's shrill voice cuts through the conversation.

There is so much fear etched into that one little word.

We turn towards Sam.

She's holding a piece of paper. A weathered, yellow piece of paper from an old journal. All too familiar red ink stains the lines on the page.

Her hands tremble as she juts the page forward.

"Did the note look like this?"

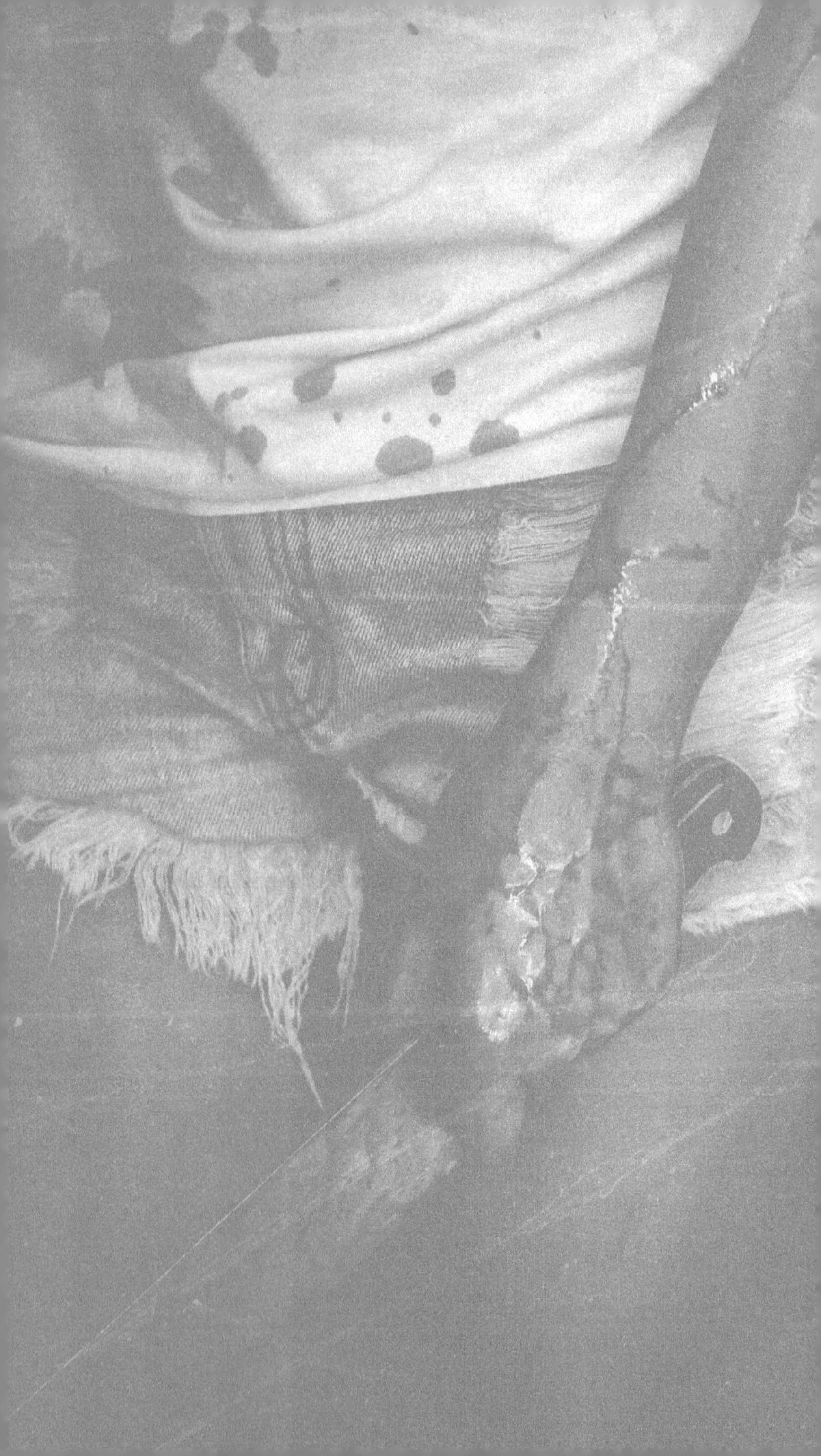

TEN

Bright red stares back at us like a haunted warning. The words scrawled across the page are as jagged as my breathing.

Eenie, meenie, miney, mo. Who wants to be the first to go?

I was so sure that Jason was the one who put that note in my room. The way his skin paled at the sight of the piece of paper has me second guessing that theory. Plus, he's not literarily inclined enough to think of a rhyme like that.

Sam is trembling on her feet. Colton runs his hands through his hair, at a loss for words. We all stare into the red oblivion completely lost at what this means. When we found the mask, the cops seemed pretty certain there was no danger. They were shockingly very nonchalant about it.

That provided us a sense of false security, but we should have known better. This town has a history of bad luck. Even if it's not the normal "hunting season" for The Senior Slayer, the mask was a warning and we were too stupid to listen.

I was too stupid to listen.

I reach out with a steady hand to pick up the tattered note. Holding the page to the ceiling, the red ink glows under the lights. I don't know what I'm searching for at this moment. I know from experience that The Senior Slayer doesn't leave any traces behind except for the occasional mask as a calling card. He makes himself known on his terms. If I hadn't seen him with my own eyes, I would've assumed it was all a superstition. Town gossip that had twisted the original killings into serial killer lore. A boogie man dressed up in a skull mask and bloodied words etched into history.

In one swift movement, Colton snatches the note from my hand.

"That's enough of that." He walks over to a random drawer near the back door and discards the paper into its depths.

He turns back towards us, remaining in the corner. He points in the direction of where Jason and I are standing.

"You two. We're not done with our gossip session. However, there's more important things to worry about right now besides that stupid prank. For all we know, it was already there before we called the cops. We can wait until morning to call them back out."

I roll my eyes at him. "It's not a prank, Colton." My voice is deadpan as I cross my arms in front of me. Jason stills beside me, but doesn't acknowledge the comment.

He holds his arms up. "Weird sex game. Whatever it is,

it can wait. Tyler called me while I was out grilling. He said a huge storm popped up over Lake Michigan and it's expected to hit pretty hard tonight. Like, severe weather warnings and power outages."

"Why does your brother care? Severe weather is normal this time of year in Graveslake," Sam says, rubbing her arms together like she's chilled to the bone.

"Because if anything happens to this cabin while we're here, he's the one who has to fix it. Mom and Dad don't like having outside workers on the grounds. It's easier to have Tyler do the work since that's his job," Colton says.

"All that money and your parents can't find someone trustworthy enough to care after a cabin that's empty ninety percent of the year? Or set up a decent security system? First world problems," Sam jabs, sending him a pointed look.

Sighing, Colton pinches the bridge of his nose. He's silent. A wry smile spreads across Sam's face. Her hip pushes out with her hand resting on her side as she watches the turmoil brew inside of him. She knows she hit a nerve and is ready to have this fight, especially after finding that note. It's clear that whatever safeguards the family have in place are useless, which is surprising giving the amount of money they have. They're either arrogant enough to think they're untouchable or so disconnected from reality to think the bare minimum will suffice.

First world problems, indeed, Sam.

Normally, Colton avoids the topic of his family's money. Even though they're basically royalty in town, being founders and all, he doesn't make the generational wealth his personality. We had plenty of rich kids who ran through our school and wore it like a badge of honor. They'd walk the halls like they paid for the tile floors we walked on and turned up their perfectly sculpted noses to anyone they didn't deem worthy. Except Colton. Colton, our big, humble, sometimes-too-naïve-for-his-own-good, teddy bear cared more about making a name for himself than riding the legacy he came from.

That doesn't stop Sam from humbling him from time to time. I guess an alleged killer hiding in the shadows doesn't excuse Colton from her loving reminders not everyone lives like he does.

"Sam, can we please not do the whole *eat the rich* shit right now? This is serious," Colton huffs.

"I'm also being serious," She quips.

"Fine." Colton throws his hands up, clearly exasperated. "Yes, my family has a lot of money. No, they don't have good security out here or a caretaker because Tyler and I would do it for them in exchange for using the cabin whenever we want. That's why we could come up here every summer. No allowance. No special treatment. So, if you could drop the damn attitude that'd be great. Happy?"

Sam holds Colton's stare for a few seconds before she starts giggling uncontrollably. Colton stares at her, brows furrowed and lips down turned. Jason and I look at each other, exchanging a look.

"You're so easy to rile up, Colt. Obviously, I know that, but it's fun to bring you back to reality every once in a while. Yes, I'm happy. Now, what do we need to do to prep for this storm?"

Colton gawks at Sam for a few seconds, face blank, before doubling over. Laughter erupts from deep inside him and fills the room, shifting the atmosphere. I can feel Jason relax beside me. A muffled snicker escapes his lips before he's laughing alongside Colton.

I shake my head at Sam, biting my bottom lip with my teeth as I stifle a laugh.

"That was good, Sam," I whisper in approval.

Sam throws me a megawatt smile, hands placed proudly at her hips.

"Someone had to break the tension. Now," she claps her hands together, "the storm."

Colton attempts to collect himself, dragging his hands down his face.

"You're on my shitlist, girl. The weekend is young," he says.

Sam blows him a kiss and winks. "Bring it, big boy."

Colton squares his shoulders and takes a breath before continuing.

"Okay. So, the cabin is pretty sturdy for a big storm. We've only had to replace a few windows from that one storm back in 2014 that destroyed the north side of town. The biggest thing to prep now is knowing where the flashlights are and making sure the generator is good to go."

"We can raid your dad's safe for a few weapons, too." Jason says beside me.

Sam rolls her eyes, saying nothing.

"Normally, those are off limits, but might be necessary given the mask and the notes. Jason, you know where it is. That's your job," Colton says as he turns to Sam. "I know you don't approve of guns, but we're going to have one out to be safe. You do not need to use it, unless you feel comfortable."

"Just because I don't approve of gun violence, doesn't mean I won't blow a hole in a fucker trying to put a knife through my chest," Sam says, flipping her hair over her shoulder.

Now it's my turn to gawk because that's the most

ridiculous thing I've ever heard her say. Sam sticks her tongue out at me.

"Sam and I can get all the candles and flashlights. We should probably plug our phones in, too, in case we lose power and landline service," I offer. "When is the storm supposed to hit?"

Above us, the lights flicker. We look up before the dimming sky lights up in a flash of white. Thunder cracks into the approaching darkness, sounds of crinkling metal and shaking glass reverberate throughout the cabin. The rumbling shakes everything it touches. Everyone startles. Sam gasps, grabbing her heart as if she's having a heart attack. Both boys duck and cover their heads like they're taking fire. I shrink into myself at the unexpected explosion.

"Fuck," I whisper. We all watch each other, holding our breaths, waiting for another crack.

Stillness grows between us. My heart is hammering in my chest. Numbness floats over my skin as adrenaline rushes through my body.

The quietness is more deafening than the thunder itself.

After a solid minute waiting to see if Mother Nature will throw another temper tantrum, the light melody of pitter-patter against the roof replaces the silence. One by one, we all collect ourselves.

"Surprise," Colton says, clearing his throat. "The storm's here."

TIME TO DIE

ELEVEN

Blackness blankets the cabin windows. The distorted sound of rain against the roof echoes into the space. Flashes of white sporadically break through the darkness. What would've been a beautiful sunset has been engulfed by the looming storm.

Colton stares out the kitchen window, frowning.

"It wasn't predicted to hit until midnight," he grumbles. "Get started here. I'm checking the generator now before the rain gets worse. It'll only power the flood lights, HVAC, and appliances, but it's better than nothing. There's a multi-charger in the living room. If you need anything else, it'll be in the office by the safe."

"We probably shouldn't split up. That's like, rule number one of serial killer movies," I say.

Colton rolls his eyes. "I'll be back in less than five minutes."

He tosses me his phone while crossing to the back door. Digging through the drawer closets to the back door, Colton retrieves one of the flashlights. He opens the door, covering his head with his arm, and makes his way outside to fulfill his duties.

Jason drops his phone on the counter before he stalks off to do his due diligence. He says nothing as he leaves, not even looking in my direction as he sulks out of the kitchen. I really can't read him right now. First, he was clearly taunting me and ready to risk it all for a joke. Next, he's acting like he's seeing a dead body for the first time.

Pussy.

Either he's really good at putting on a show or he seriously didn't know about the note in my room. I'll torture or tease it out of him later. There's still time to have my revenge.

"Can you plug mine in, too? Just to be safe?" Sam asks, placing her phone next to Jason's.

Sam busies herself by opening all the cabinets to find our supplies. I collect all of our phones before making my way to the living room. I wander through the space, looking at each outlet along the walls, until I finally spot the charging station tucked neatly behind the entryway table. I take note of everyone's battery level as I plug in each phone, until I notice a message from an unknown number on Jason's phone.

(702) 059 - 1980

Do your job before I do it for you

I put the phone back in its spot and busy myself with the others. Not even two minutes later, the phone buzzes again atop the wooden surface. I toss a glance back at it. A new text message from the same number flashes across the screen. Being the nosy bitch I am, I pick it up to peek at the message.

You have until Monday. I'll be watching.

My lips curl in on themselves as I purse them together. Seems like there's trouble in model paradise. That's one thing I'm grateful for, being an independent author. I don't have anyone to report to besides my editor. I don't have some big publishing house breathing down my neck when I don't meet a deadline. Plus, I don't have a PR team to scold me when I'm being too risque. I made my pen name off of being controversial. That's never going to change.

Returning the phone to its designated spot on the table, I saunter back to the kitchen. I'll let him find those messages on his own time. We have more pressing issues to deal with at the moment.

Sam already has various supplies scattering the counter top upon my return. We work together as she hums her favorite song. Batteries, flashlights, candles, matches—everything we'll need to keep the metaphorical lights on until morning. Bad weather is common in Graveslake, especially late summer. Dark, ominous clouds cover the sky with their rumbling music. Very rarely do the storms turn into something severe, but when they do, it's serious. Better to be safe than sorry, especially since we're allegedly being stalked by a serial killer.

A few minutes pass as we work to the tune of *Ballyhoo!*. I catch Sam looking at me out of the corner of my eye. I stop putting together the flashlight in my hand and look at her. The expression on her face is smugness mixed with curiosity.

I stare at her for a few seconds, trying to figure out what her problem is.

"What?" I clip out.

Sam smirks and shrugs.

"Oh, nothing, baby girl. I just thought maybe you wanted to clue me in on your big secret before I figure it out for myself."

I roll my eyes at her and return to my flashlight that refuses to screw back together.

"There's literally nothing to tell. Jason is being a dick."

Sam nods next to me.

"Mhm. Sure. And you're sure that he is *being* a dick, not *giving you* his dick?"

The flashlight clatters to the counter after I fumble it out of my hands. I curse under my breath. Slumping into the high top stool next to me, I bury my face in my hands.

Sam watches me, not saying a word, letting me process how I want to have this conversation. I rub my fingers across my temples and down the sides of my face. My mouth opens a few times, but nothing comes out. How do I tell her what happened? It wasn't wrong, but it definitely wasn't planned.

"I...well...um," I stammer. Sam tilts her chin and crosses her arms.

I clear my throat, sitting up straighter.

"I'm not going to lie to you. This stays between us. Girl to girl. I'm serious!" I say, looking around to ensure the guys haven't returned yet.

Sam nods, still silent.

"Okay," I breathe out. "Soooo, hypothetically, maybe Jason was in my room after my shower. Maybe he cornered me. Maybeeeee he kissed me. And maybe hemademecum-betterthananyoneelse," I blurt out.

Sam raises both eyebrows at me, eyes bug-eyed. A smile creeps across her face. She's nodding at me.

Smug little shit.

"You've got that look on your face. What?" I ask.

Sam shrugs, schooling her face back to a cooled expression, then begins picking up the candles in front of her. She starts making her way towards the living room before responding.

"I knew it. I just wanted to hear you say it," she throws back over her shoulder.

I scramble off my stool to follow her.

"What the hell do you mean, '*you knew?*'" I ask.

Sam starts placing candles around the room in quick succession. I'm standing in the middle of the living room, following her in a circle.

"I mean, I know. It's clear there's something between the two of you. It's been obvious for years. I just knew you put the health of your friendship before your love life. That's why you go on those sexcapades while on your book tours. It's safer for you than expressing your true feelings."

I gape at her, speechless. Did she really just psychoanalyze me like Dr. Phil?

"That's...that's ridiculous. Jason might be conventionally attractive, and have a great body, and maybe his dick is the best boyfriend dick I've seen, but that doesn't mean I've always had a thing for him," I argue, crossing my arms and biting my lip.

Sam turns around, pointing a manicured nail at my pose.

"That, right there, proves you're lying," she says.

I drop my arms immediately. I look everywhere else except at her, avoiding the reality of this discussion. Sam comes over and grabs my hands. She squeezes them in her warm grasp. Her slender fingers pull my chin to turn my face towards her own. Her smile is soft and reassuring as she holds my gaze.

"If it's the truth, it's okay. I'll still love you like a sister. I'll support whatever crazy decision you make. I only want you to be honest with yourself," she says, squeezing my hand in hers.

I take a few deep breaths, standing there with her, hand in hand. I can never express how grateful I am for her friendship. She truly is the beautiful sunshine in my dark, little world and I love her for it.

I close my eyes and take a steady inhale.

"Fine. Yes, there's something between us. I just don't know what," I say breathlessly.

Sam drops my hands, jumping up and down in front of me.

"I knew it!" She laughs, wrapping me in a hug. "I've been *waiting* for this day to happen. Finally."

I grimace at her assumption, but hug her back. Laughing along with her, I shake my head at her cute, little dramatics. She's so adorable when she gets excited about happy things.

"You don't look happy, though," she observes, holding me at arm's length.

"Because Jason thinks he can bully me into submission. You know damn well that's not how my relationships usually go," I say.

Sam shrugs before wandering off to finish finding new homes for her candles.

"I'm not saying that you don't deserve to be put in your place. You've always given him shit. However, if you want to be on top," she turns back to give me a wicked grin, "then you need to beat him at his own game. Stop being *Ashe, the friend* and be *Ashe, the horror goddess.*"

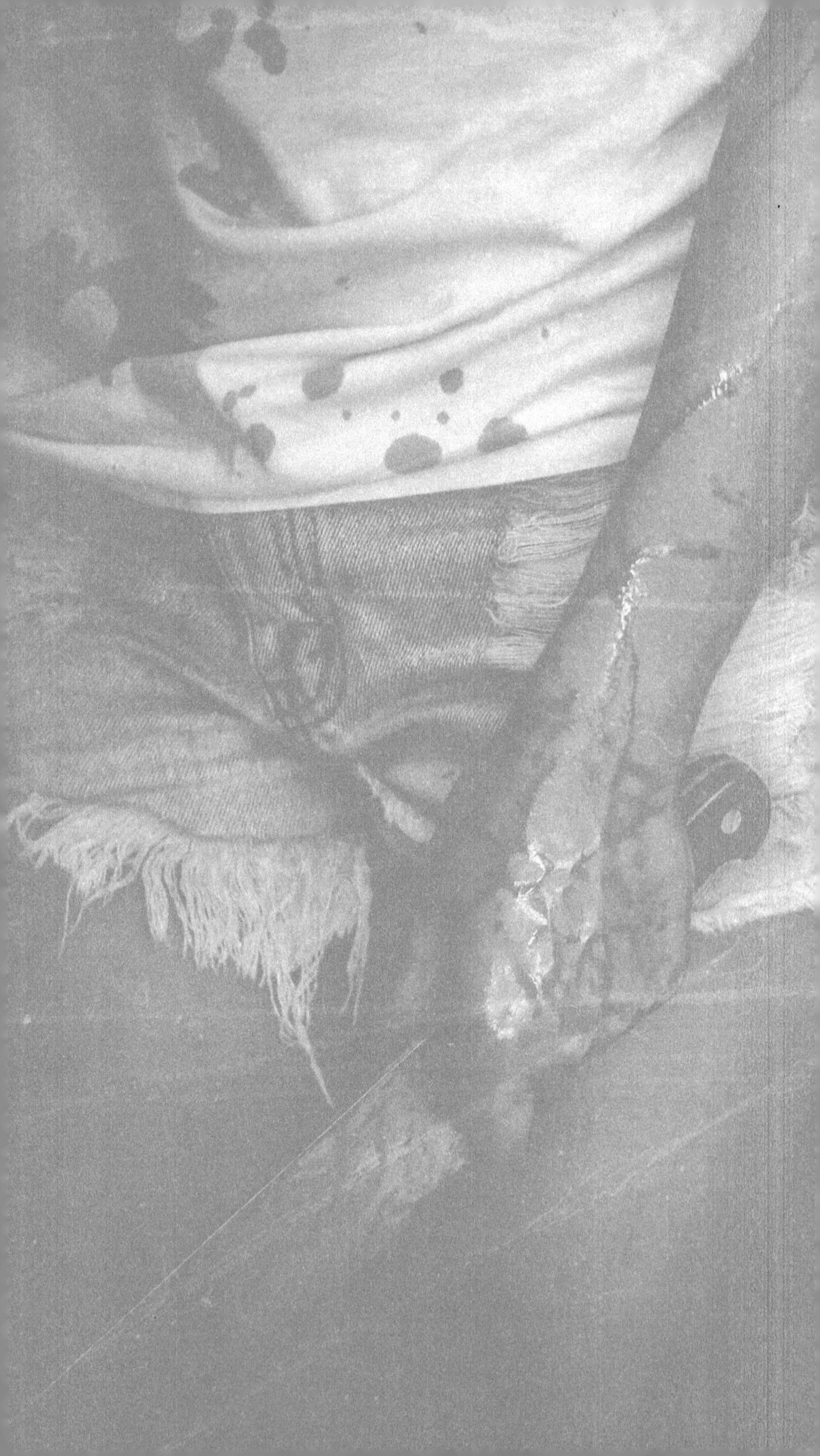

TWELVE

Within the hour, the main room of the cabin is glowing like the set of *The Elvira Show*. Candles littered the room, the innocent flames flickering shadows across the walls. If there wasn't the looming danger of death, it would be quite beautiful.

Both boys are still absent, working on their designated tasks for the evening.

So much for, *"I'll be back in less than five minutes."*

With nothing else to occupy our racing thoughts, Sam and I decide it's time to start a fire. One by one, we place the logs into the hearth until a crude box is formed. I find some old newspapers in the kitchen to use for kindling. Retrieving her lighter from the deck, Sam lights the yellowed paper until every inch is covered by the orange warmth.

Sam sits, curled up on the couch, across from the fireplace. Her blanket wraps around her like a cocoon as she scans whatever reading material she found in the library. Normally, she'd be doomscrolling on TikTok during times like this. Her favorite way to disassociate. But since we're expected to lose power at some point, she decided to save her phone for later.

"I rather keep it where I need it than drain the battery. With my luck, the power would go out the minute I go to plug it back in and it dies," she had said in passing, searching for a book to read.

I envy her ability to disconnect so easily. I haven't been able to sit still, pacing back and forth in front of the fireplace and picking at my cuticles. Ever since the second note was found, my brain has been running faster than the final girl of a horror movie. While the option that the person leaving us cryptic messages is some crazy kid who found their way back here, it's not likely. It's also not likely that it's Colton or Jason, based on both of their reactions earlier in the kitchen. The little gremlin in the back of my head is screaming at me. I know the answer I'm looking for. The problem is, I don't want it to be true.

Jason. Fucking Jason.

That's another problem I need to take care of. I let him get into my head. That shy, little girl that everyone knew in high school died the same night Tristan did. I need to remember that. If Jason wants to get into bed with me, then so be it. It's just another notch in the headboard of simple men who think they can throw me around. Most of them don't expect the dominating goddess that emerges once the door closes. Jason doesn't know what I've gone through to create the new person I am. Only two people know that answer and one of them is dead.

I turn on my heels to continue my monotonous circle.

There's no way The Senior Slayer is here. It's outside of hunting season. Killers like him have a specific M.O. He's never deviated from his pattern before...before me.

Reaching the end of the fireplace, I pause, picking at my right thumb. A small piece of stray cuticle hangs from beneath my nail. Gingerly, I place the piece of skin between my front teeth. I bite down and pull as copper lingers on my lips. Removing my hand from my mouth, I look down at my thumb. The hang nail is gone, now replaced by a dribble of blood oozing from the side. I frown, scolding myself. It's a bad, anxious habit I can't shake. Wrapping my thumb with the hem of my shirt, I make another turn to continue my march in front of the fireplace.

Technically speaking, I *am* the finalist of final girls. The one that got away. The one that beat the system. I've been living under false pretenses as an up and coming author who struck it big on BookTok. No one knows *why* I am obsessed over these crimes. No one knows my close encounter with the phantom menace changed my brain chemistry, permanently reliving that day in my head. I began writing to stop the Rolodex of chilling memories in my head as a futile attempt to understand his motives. Slowly, the darkness seeped into every crevice of my mind, leeching its bloody mark into every aspect of my life. It was exhausting keeping the inner voices quiet while constantly looking over my shoulder, waiting for the other shoe to drop. Eventually, the only way to find peace was to shove out the noise and lock the demoness away, only allowing her out to play with willing partners.

Reaching, yet again, the far side of the wall, I stop. A heavy sigh leaves my lips. My hands anxiously clap together. Out of the corner of my eye, I can see Sam glancing up from her book. A single eyebrow is raised, but she remains silent. I tap my feet while keeping beat with my hands. Anxiety bubbles up from the pit of my stomach. Sam clears her throat and throws me another glance.

"Wanna talk about it?" she asks.

I tap the tops of my fingers together for a few seconds, contemplating how to answer that question. I could tell her I'm the reason there's potentially a homicidal maniac out to get us. I could also tell her my obsession to get back at Jason simmers just under that bubbly pit of rabid anxiety.

I nod my head, but no words come out.

Sam continues to stare at me, waiting for a response.

"I just— Do you ever— What I'm trying to say—," I say, stumbling over my words.

Sam purses her lips together.

"You're really shaken up over all this, huh?" she asks, amusement lacing each word. She places a hand in front of her face to conceal her giggling, the gentle shake of her shoulders giving away her attempts.

I shoot a glare at her. She holds her hands up.

"Forget it. Why aren't the guys back yet?" I ask.

She shrugs her shoulders before returning to her book.

"Your guess is as good as mine, babes," she says.

I grumble to myself, scanning the glass doors to the deck. The heavy rain blocks out any sort of view beyond the three feet illuminated by the flood lights. Darkness engulfs the trees just beyond the cabin. The sense that someone is watching puts my nerves on edge. The flight or flight part of my bird brain picks at my insides to take control. I mentally push it down.

A pile of red catches my attention. The table to the right of the doors is cluttered with supplies we had stockpiled for tonight. I don't remember finding a red flashlight. Wandering over, the object comes into view. It's Jason's shibari rope. Tracing the figure eight wrapping of the rope, a thought occurs to me.

Excitement replaces the pit of despair in my stomach.

The corners of my mouth round upward as I grip the bundle in my hand.

"Sam. I'm going to find Jason," I say. "Someone needs to make sure that idiot didn't accidentally lock himself in the safe."

Sam snorts, not looking up from her reading.

Turning to walk towards the stairs, I hear Sam call after me.

"Don't do anything I wouldn't do," she says.

Oh, you sweet, sweet summer child.

THIRTEEN

A soft glow emanates from the end of the hallway. Shuffles and shakes of something metallic echo off the walls as I get closer. Once I reach the door, I peer through the opening. Jason is standing at the desk at the far side of the room with the safe clearly open. Bags and hunting clothing are strewn about the space; some laying over the green, upholstered high-back chair in the corner, some hanging over the safe door. Jason's back is to me. His focus remains on the weaponry in front of him.

I slide the door open an inch with my index finger, testing the hinges to see if they'll give away my position. Satisfied with the silence that follows, I place my right palm flat against the door's surface. My other hand hovers over the doorknob, a precautionary stance in case I need to catch the door from swinging into the room. Pushing it open enough to slide through, I inch my way into the space and slowly close the door behind me. The click of the lock is indistinguishable from the metallic ticks of the weapons Jason is currently handling.

My heart hammers in my chest. Excitement fizzes up from the pit that was filled with dread moments earlier. The red rope hangs off my right shoulder and the pocket knife I hid away in my room is stored in my back pocket. A warning and a promise. I keep my eyes laser focused on the center of Jason's back as I inch my way closer to him. Each step is met with soft, shallow breaths. Stalking and binding isn't my first choice in getting someone to submit, but it'll do for today. Experimenting makes relationships stronger, right?

Standing mere inches behind him, I carefully pull the rope from my side. Wrapping the rope around, I quickly create the makeshift restraints I'll need for someone his size. Jason is totally obvious to my presence. Glorious back muscles flex and contract under his dark shirt as he continues his methodical preparation of supplies. The room is filled with metallic clicks, the scent of gunpowder, and a promise of redemption.

I wait until Jason's finished with the current rifle in his hand before I make my move. The minute the gun clacks down on the desktop, I jump at his back. A circle of red rope swiftly finds its way around his neck. My hands grip the rope nearest to his exposed skin, fingers digging into my palms to ensure I don't lose my grip. I pull down quickly to find my footing. Jason stiffens before his instincts kick in.

"What the fuck is this?" he chokes out.

His hands fly to the rope around his neck, frenzied to free himself. He tries to reach around to see who his assailant is, but those all too delicious muscles hinder his mobility. I stay just out of reach behind him. A lioness ready to take her prey. Hearing Jason struggle against my restraints only makes me more feral. My core warms at the thought of having him submit to me. I stuff back a moan, remaining focused on my plan.

I wrap the rope around my hands before pulling back again. Jason stumbles from the jolt. The lack of air makes his attempts to escape weak with each panicked breath. I yank again and push my right foot into the backs of his legs as he buckles to his knees.

A low, seductive laugh rises from deep inside me. *This* is what I live for.

Desperation.

Total loss of control.

Totally *mine.*

"Who the hell do you think you are?" Jason sputters. He pries at the rope around his neck. A subtle, pink glow forms around the spot where red fiber meets skin. Keeping the tightness in the restraint, I place one foot on the pressure point of his right calf and push. Can't have him getting away from me so soon. Jason gasps at the contact. I lean forward, grazing my breasts against his shoulder blades, nipples hardening under the contact. My lips brush past his ear.

"Your worst nightmare or your greatest pleasure," I whisper. My tongue glides from his lobe to the tip of his ear and I nip at the cartilage. Jason hisses between clenched teeth.

"Ashe? Seriously? Are you crazy?" he asks. His body is still, waiting to figure out my next move.

I pull him back against me and he chokes under the pressure of the rope. His posture starts to falter, most likely from lack of oxygen. I only need to burn ninety more seconds before he passes out and I can start phase two.

"Crazy is an understatement," I deadpan. "You started this. I'm just finishing it."

79. 78. 77. 76...

A snort, more resembling a gurgle, escapes his throat. He writhes against the restraints, slumping forward slightly.

57. 56. 55. 54...

"Let me go and I'll show you how to finish. You seemed to like it the first time," he groans.

33. 32. 31. 30...

I snort against his neck, inhaling his scent. It's heady against the stirring excitement. I steady my breath, pushing down my growing arousal. I lean back from him and adjust my grip one last time.

18. 17. 16. 15...

"That's not how this works. You wanted to know my secret. Well, here it is. Welcome to the freak show, Jason. Let's have some fun," I purr.

4. 3. 2. 1...

I give one final squeeze before Jason slumps over onto the floor.

It takes me a few minutes, but I manage to drag his body over to the chair.

Sitting him up right, I make quick work to tie his arms and legs to the appropriate sides of the furniture's feet. Standing back, I take a look at my handiwork. He's seated like a beautiful statue. His clothed front fully exposed to whatever I want. A calmness takes over my body.

I'm back in control.

I saunter over to him, crawling onto his lap. I straddle his legs, my center placed delicately above his. Placing my hands on his chest, I stare at his chiseled features. His chest slowly rises and falls under my touch. Not how I expected our first, or even second, intimate interaction to go. In the back of my mind, I was hoping to make it more normal.

I trace the outline of his face with my fingers, pushing a stray piece of raven hair off his forehead.

Oh, well.

I grab his chin between my thumb and fingers. Gently, I shake his head. When he doesn't stir, I tap his cheek with my finger tips. It takes a few tries before his eyes flutter back to life. Gasping, he takes a huge breath. His eyes dart around the room before landing on me.

"There he is. Welcome back to the living, baby," I coo at him, caressing his cheek with the back of my fingers. I flutter my lashes and feign my sweetest smile possible.

Jason's whole body juts forward as he tries to move, which he quickly finds is useless. The chair beneath us groans under the sudden movement. He looks around again, lips pursed in a thin line. I can see the wheels turning in his mind as he tries to work his way out of this one.

I giggle. His eyes shoot back to me, glaring and heated.

"You're cute when you're all worked up," I say, gently running my fingers through his hair from the top of his forehead. His head follows, a deep rumbling escaping from him. I watch as his jaw relaxes ever so slightly. Making my way to the crown of his skull, I ball my hand into his hair, pulling his gaze back to me. His eyes lock with mine with a burning desire behind them. He either wants to fuck me or fucking kill me. Either will do in this scenario.

"What do you want, Ashe," he asks. His voice is low and

gravely, no doubt from the rope choking him moments earlier. Strangling someone can do a number on their windpipe if you don't do it correctly.

"I told you. I want to have fun," I say, innocently tipping my head to one side. I bite my bottom lip to contain my excitement.

He pulls at his restraints, bucking his hips into me. His noticeably hard length presses into my center. The contact sends a jolt of energy straight to my core. I tilt my head back and push back, savoring the sensation. One hand gripping his hair and the other keeping steady on his chest, I roll my hips forward to meet his growing erection.

"Be a good girl and let me out of these restraints. I'll show you how much *fun* we can have," he grunts.

I cluck my tongue, continuing my slow roll over him. "Good girls do as they're told."

I lean in, pressing my chest to his. I pull his head forward. Our lips are inches apart and I can feel his warm breath mixing with my own.

"I am neither good nor a girl. I am a woman. Women take what they want and leave you begging like the little bitch you are. You took my control away from me with that little stunt you pulled. I want it back. So you're going to be a good little pet and give me what I want."

"And what if I don't?" Jason bites.

I release his head and capture his face, closing the distance between us. My mouth feathers along his as I drag my tongue along his bottom lip. His mouth opens slightly, tongue darting out to meet mine. I snicker. His impatience glaringly obvious in his actions.

"Your body says otherwise," I mew before taking his mouth on mine. Lips crash together with fervent need.

He groans against me as I lick his bottom lip, asking for

entrance. He opens, fully submitting to my request. Our tongues dance together as I grind over his covered length. His sweet taste, pineapple and rum, invades my senses as I deepen the kiss. I pull his lip between my teeth, biting hard until copper laces my tongue. I lean back and smile as blood drips from my mouth. Wiping the blood away with my thumb, I remove the knife from my waistband with my other hand. I guide it gingerly under the front of his shirt. Blade facing up and tip firmly against his toned abs, Jason stills beneath me.

"You're just a fuck toy to me. A warm, living dildo that I can have my way with," I say, setting the knife taught against his shirt.

Jerking up, I rip his shirt with ease from waist to neck. The shirt falls open to reveal smooth, sweat-soaked skin. I glide the tip of the knife down Jason's cheek before placing it at the base of his throat. Jason's eyes widen, but he stays silent, watching every movement.

"Now, be a good pet and sit still. Wouldn't want your pretty face to get ruined," I croon. Keeping the knife tightly at his neck, I slide my free hand beneath his waistband. My fingers trace the outline of his swollen member and Jason's hips tilt towards my touch.

"Tsk, tsk, tsk. So needy," I taunt. My fingers continue to trace from base to tip. I flick my thumb over his swollen head, wetness covering my skin.

"What's the safe word, pet?" I demand.

"Get. Fucked," Jason spits back.

I grab his hard cock in my hand and squeeze, applying enough pressure to make him hiss from the contact.

"Try again," I chide. "What. Is. The. Safe. Word?"

I can feel his heartbeat hammering inside his chest. The rise and fall of his breathing becomes more erratic. I tighten my grip on him even more, staring into the burning frustration behind his amber eyes.

Seconds pass between us. The stare off continues, challenging the other one to break. After a few breaths, I get what I want.

"Slayer," he breathes.

Triumph spreads across my face. My insides clench at his submission, pussy wet and waiting to finally feel him inside me.

"Good boy," I muse, ripping his pants down low. I look down as I pull him free. Licking my lips, I take in the sight of him. His impressive length throbs in my hand, beckoning to me to feel him inside.

I push myself off of Jason's lap, releasing his dick from my grasp. I place the knife on the side table next to us before returning to stand in front of him.

"Where are my manners?" I ask, gesturing to myself. "Let's remove these clothes before we get to the good stuff."

Slowly, I drag my oversized shirt over my head, letting my breasts catch on the hem. They bounce ever so slightly as I toss the shirt to the floor. Turning around, I run my hands over my curves. I hook my fingers into the hem of my shorts and slowly bend over as I drag them down my toned legs, careful to give a full view of my soaked center to him.

A whispered, "Fuck," comes from behind me as I reach the floor. I look back to see Jason gripping the arms of the chair, his cock standing at full attention. His tip glistens in precum, ready and waiting for me.

Sauntering back over to him, I straddle his legs, tucking my knees between his thighs and the arm rests. Jason's eyes wander over my naked frame. His jaw remains tense.

Leaning back, I glide my hand down between us. My fingers play over my clit, tracing a circle around the aroused bud. My hips rock against his length as I continue to tease myself. A deep, primal growl emanates from Jason.

"Come on, Ashe," he begs. He rolls his head back releasing a sigh.

"Not so powerful now, are you?" I sing.

I move to position him at my center, wet and aching for him. I grab his hair, yanking him back to my gaze. Painstakingly slow, I lower myself onto him. His eyes widen, ablaze with desire. My jaw drops open at the contact.

"Oh, yes," I moan as my hips lower fully onto him. The fullness overtakes my senses. I take a second to savor how he touches every part of me.

Fuck, I've had a good lay before, but I've never felt anyone who felt *this* good. It's like he was made for me.

Taking a steadying breath, I pull myself back up his length. My pussy spasms at the contact as I tease myself with his swollen head. I slide my hips back down again. Jason bucks his hips to meet mine with what little give he has in his restraints.

"Tisk, tisk. Be patient, pet. Let me have my fun and then you can cum for me."

"Fucking hell, little bat," he groans, leaning his head back with eyes closed. I roll my hips clockwise and he groans even louder. My insides clench tighter at the primal sound. I pick up my hips again to find a rhythm as I ride him.

"Look at you, being a good little fuck toy for me. Show me how much you love this," I tease.

Jason brings his head back to my body and dips to nip at the skin at my collar bone. His tongue runs along the edge of the sensitive ridge, making me lean into his touch.

"Shall I show you like this?" My nipples brush against

his neck and he takes the opportunity to take them into his mouth.

"Mmmmm, good girl." His teeth bite into my sensitive mounds and I cry out at the beautiful pain.

"That's not how this works," I grind out, shoving his face off of me and holding him to the back of the chair. Electricity races through my body, emboldening my assault on his cock. Pumping faster, I move my free hand back to my clit. Circling the tender bud with my index finger, I can feel myself building. High on everything happening all at once, I don't notice Jason returning his mouth on my nipples.

"Fuck, yes. Keep doing that, Jason," I whimper, leaning into him.

I can feel Jason smile into my skin as he continues his attention to my breasts. Sucking, licking, biting the tender skin within his reach. I cry out as he takes my other nipple into his mouth and bites down. His tongue laps at the tender flesh as a warmness radiates from the center of my breast. A static tingle runs over my skin. Jason continues to suck while I impale myself over and over again. When he pulls back, his grin is coated with a red tinge. A color I recognize all too well.

Blood drips from his bottom lip.

My breath hitches. Seeing him commit to my darkest fantasy sends me over the edge.

"Fuck this," I hiss, reaching over the side of the chair to retrieve the knife.

"What are you doing," he asks, warily.

Slowing my pace to a gentle roll, I carefully cut Jason's hands free from the sides of the chair.

"Don't act stupid. It's not cute," I say, dropping the knife behind him. It clatters against the floor. I grab Jason's face between my hands and lean in. Our lips are barely touching. Our breathing mixes together into a heady concoction of lust and desire.

Jason cautiously raises his hands to grab my hips. His fingertips dig into my sides. He slaps my ass, the contact echoing through the room. I throw my head back as I cry out at the pain. My skin warms under his touch. I begin to pump my hips faster, feeling my insides clench again so close to the edge.

"Not stupid," he grunts out. "Tell me what you want."

I stop my momentum. I look at him through hooded eyes.

"Fuck me like you hate me," I say before kissing him.

Our mouths crash together again. We're breathless as we consume each other.

Jason tightens his grip on my hips again, matching my pace. His hips drill into me as he drags me up and down his wicked length. Kissing, biting, grabbing each other in need. It's a frenzy of emotions and actions as we devour each other.

My ass bounces to a rhythm as I find my release. My pussy gripping him as I scream into his shoulder.

"Oh, fuck! Yes, please! Yes! Fuck, Jason!"

Jason wraps his arms around me, continuing to pump into me. Each thrust harder and deeper than the next. I can feel him stiffen inside me as he finds his own release.

"Oh, fuckkkk," he bellows.

Jason's hips buck into me as he fills me. His cock twitching with every last drop he has to offer. Spent of all my energy, I drop into his embrace. I nuzzle my face into the crook of his neck. Still inside me, Jason holds me against him, one hand on my ass while the other plays with my hair splayed across his chest. Our breathing slows in tandem.

Jason's body vibrates beneath me as I hear a laugh rumble through his chest. He doesn't say anything as he leans in to kiss my forehead, this time his lips lingering against my damp skin. As twisted and unconventional our quasi-relationship is, *this* is what I've been missing in my life. The connection. The trust. The mutual respect. No one else has matched my twisted energy like Jason.

We remain twisted together for what feels like forever. He peppers kisses across my skin as I bask in his worship of me. Murmurs of perfection, beauty, and wit all mixed into one.

The afterglow bliss fills the room around us. Lights flicker against my eyelids leaving white sparks in my vision. I lean deeper into Jason's embrace, relishing the warmth radiating off of his body. Nothing could get better than this moment.

The lower flicker of light continues until everything is dark behind my eyelids. Jason sighs against me. "Damn it," he mutters.

He rocks me gently. I look up to see the outline of his body against the moonlight. He smiles at me sheepishly.

"The power finally gave out."

TIME TO DIE

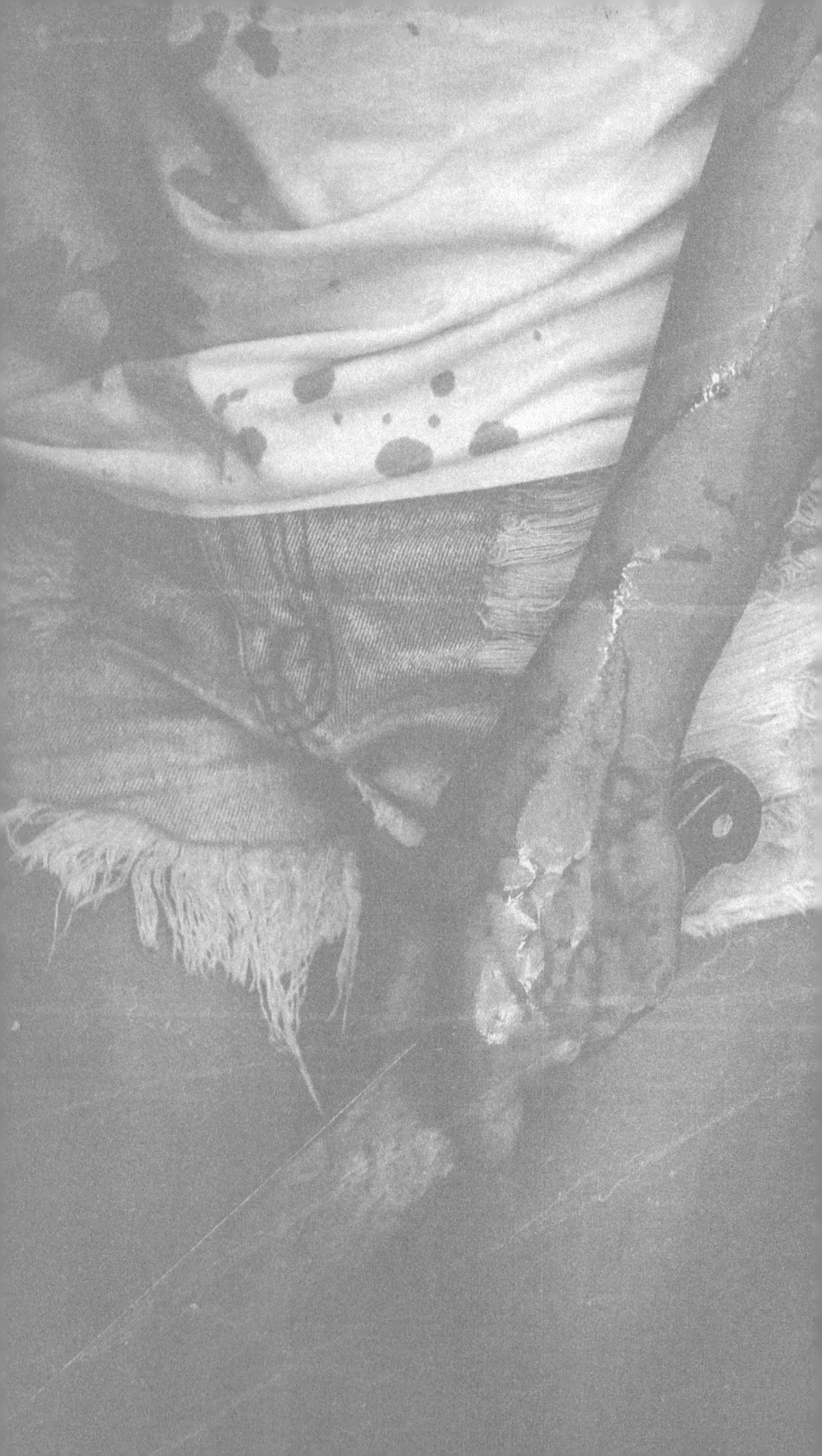

FOURTEEN

We dressed quickly before making our way back to the living room. Opening the office door, we exit our blissful sanctuary into the dark unknown. Jason takes the lead, carefully tiptoeing down the hallway. He holds my hand behind his back so I can navigate through the darkness. Our soft steps echo into the distance. It's unnervingly quiet.

Too quiet.

The moment the thought crosses my mind, a door slams behind us. I jump at the sudden noise and drop his hand while Jason barely flinches. I look back in an attempt to see which door it was.

"Probably just the wind. I left a window open in my room," he says passively.

"Okay," I respond, unsure if I believe that. I can't feel any draft coming through the narrow space.

"Sam was on the couch when I left her," I mention, still looking behind me. For a split second, I swear I can see the outline of a figure standing in the darkness at the end of the hall. I blink a few times to adjust to the darkness, but once my eyes refocus, the figure is gone. I pick up my pace to catch up to Jason. I know better than to go back and investigate on my own. Turning around, my face makes sudden contact with Jason's back. He's stopped at the entryway.

"Ouch! What the fuck, Jason?" I curse, attempting to shove him out of my way. His body barely moves under my touch. Stepping around to face him, I shake his shoulder again.

"Hello. Earth to Jason. Are you good?" I ask, standing fully in front of him.

His pallid skin is ghost white. Fear is stricken through every beautiful line of his face. His body doesn't move, but his eyes track something behind me.

"Oh my god, Jason. You act like you've seen a dead body," I quip.

Jason grabs my shoulders with a firm grip and jerks me around to face the couch. I blink my eyes to adjust to the dim light. Copper invades my nostrils before my brain can process what I'm seeing. My breathing catches as the warmth drains from my entire body.

Laid out on the couch is a body.

A bloodied, mutilated body.

A body with crimson-stained blonde hair and glossy, blue eyes.

Colton's body.

"No. No, no, no!" I cry.

Blood spills over every surface of the fabric. The red stain leeches onto the wooden floor boards in front of us. His body is seated on the middle cushion of the couch. The gray shirt he was wearing before leaving the cabin is ripped clean open. Maroon paints every inch of his exposed skin. His head is propped against the back cushion. Vacant, glassy eyes stare at us. A hallowed look across his features.

"Jason, help him," I scream, racing towards him.

Jason grabs my wrist before I can make it onto the couch.

"Ashe, no," is all he chokes out.

"What do you mean no? Do something," I say, pulling against his grasp.

I break free, falling knees first into the bloody puddle in front of us. Only inches away, I can see why Jason refused my pleas. I scramble back on instinct, my hands becoming covered in whatever gore has leeched onto the ground.

Beneath the crimson stain across Colton's chest is a deep crater. Darkness engulfs the two inch hole into nothingness. Tendrils of flesh hang from the opening, dripping the life force that was once my friend. The faint outline of something rubbery and opaque peeks through the opening. Drips of white coming from the rolled rim of the object.

Bile rises from within me as panic replaces all rational thought. I cover my mouth with both hands, a useless attempt to hold back a gag. Leaning forward into the sticky mess on the floor, I retch up everything that was consumed for the day. Bitter rum, ground beef, and the tangy hint of ketchup mixes into the gruesome scene around me. My arms shake as I attempt to hold myself back against dry heaving.

I've read about scenes like this growing up. Looked at numerous crime scene photos in my research for my stories. Hell, I've *killed* someone in real life out of survival. Yet, when faced with the reality of The Slayer's morbid curiosities, I'm no better than the average person. Nothing could have prepared me for this.

Firm pressure wraps around my abdomen. The sound around me rings. A voice echos in the distance. My vision starts to blur as my mind swims. I grab onto the pressure at my center, nails digging into flesh. In a daze, I turn back to see Jason behind me. His lips move quickly and the timber of his voice reverberates through my chest. Words drift to me like I'm underwater, muffled and slow.

"Get up, Ashe. We have to move," he says.

My body moves on autopilot. Legs under me push against the ground towards the kitchen. Feet pounding against the wooden floor. Blood rushing in my ears as my mind continues to swim under the adrenaline. I scramble to hold onto the marble counter as Jason lets me go to retrieve a flashlight. When he returns, he grabs my chin between his thumb and index finger.

"Look at me," he begs. His voice cracks, deep and gravely. I grasp onto his wrist as my eyes bore into his. My anchor into madness. The only sanity in this nightmare.

"We have to find Sam. I know you're in shock right now, but I really need badass, shit-kicking Ashe to get it together until we can get out," he says as he tightens his grip on my chin.

I blink at him processing his words.

Badass Ashe. Horror writer Ashe. Ashe *the killer.*

I can do this.

I nod my head, grabbing his hand to bring him closer to me. Our lips touch and I kiss him with a fierceness that can only be described as *goodbye.*

Everything I've done has led up to this night. All the new articles I've studied. All the books I've written off the twisted killings of this psychopath. All my success is attributed to him. I know him better than anyone else. I know how to survive, because I already did it once. The Senior Slayer doesn't act alone; they always send some poor minion to do their bidding. To take down the monster, we have to find the puppet first.

I don't want to acknowledge it, but I know deep down tonight will end very, very badly.

FIFTEEN

Jason left me in the kitchen to retrieve a few items from the safe, including a gun. He thinks it's a good way to defend ourselves. I've never held a gun before. I have no idea how to use it. In the movies, they just say point and shoot. It can't be that hard. Right?

My fingers thrum over the edge of the island as I pace around it, endlessly waiting for Jay to return. My mind is a war zone. The fear and grief over the loss of my friend threatens to pull me under, drowning over my own humanity. A stark contrast from the killer locked deep inside, banging against the box I keep it in. Red, hot anger seeps through the cracks like lava flowing from a volcano. The need for revenge swims just under the surface of sanity.

I fell victim to The Slayer once before.

I fought my way out to survive.

I thought I was safe.

I refuse to fall back into his trap.

I will not die today.

Footsteps drift through the cabin, shaking me from my spiral. I stand frozen in the center of the kitchen, eyes wide and staring into the darkness past the candle lit living room. I carefully back peddle until my back is against the stove. My hand fumbles up to the butcher's block, seeking the touch of something cold and metallic. Finding my prize, I grip the hilt and quietly draw the knife from its home. I stalk around the island with my back firmly against the marble counter. The thud of boots against the wood floor grow louder. I find my hiding spot just behind the corner of the fridge and hug the knife to my chest.

From the reflection of the back door, I can see a hooded figure approaching. I mentally count to ten in an attempt to calm my nerves. Once I see the figure step towards the fridge, I jump out. Stabbing. Clawing. Grabbing onto anything my hands can take hold. It's a worthless attempt. I'm slicing through the air. In seconds, the figure engulfs me with their body. My hands are pinned above me with my back against the fridge. The knife clatters to the ground beside me. With their other hand, the person drops the hood to reveal my attacker.

It's fucking Jason.

And he looks pissed. Fire sits behind his eyes as he glares at me.

"What in the hell do you think you're doing?" he seethes.

I open my mouth to bite back, but nothing comes out. He stays silent for a beat before sighing. Jason releases me, picking up the knife from the floor and hands it towards me.

I take the knife and inspect it in my hands.

"I didn't realize you had changed," I muttered. "My instincts took over, I'm sorry. I'm just scared."

Jason grabs my chin and pulls it up to meet his gaze. A small glimmer of empathy traces his face.

"Listen to me right now. I am fully aware that you can take care of yourself. However, I promise to not let anything happen to you. We just have to find Sam, then we can get out of here."

Something warm flutters in my chest. I stare back at Jason, searching his face for any sign of treason. There's none. Beneath that bad boy exterior is a heart of gold. It shouldn't have taken a killer for me to realize it, but I'm grateful for him, nonetheless. I safely tuck the knife in my waistband, next to the flashlight in my back pocket.

"Okay." I nod. "I trust you. Let's find Sam."

Jason's tight smile turns into a beaming grin. He intertwines my hand in his and leads us to the deck. The outdoor lights flash on, flooding the space. I squint against the blinding light. Jason releases my hand and gestures to the elevator. I give him a puzzled look before boarding the platform.

"I already checked the rooms while I went to the office. She's not here. The next plausible option is the boat shed." He closes the gate behind him and switches the panel to *down*. We descend in silence with only the hum of the night surrounding us. Trees sway in the breeze. Leaves tickling against each other. The skitter of animals against the ground. The soft crash of the lake against the dock floats through the air. The elevator clatters when it hits the ground.

Reaching for the elevator door to exit, Jason blocks me with his arm. He puts a finger to his lips, miming to me to be quiet. He points to his ear before gesturing to the darkness in front of us. We stand for a beat unmoving. Silence stretching between us and whatever is stalking us within these trees. Somewhere off in the distance I can hear the crunch of leaves.

Crunch...

Crunch...

Crunch...

The familiar cadence of footsteps.

I pull the flashlight from my back pocket and flick it on.

"Shut that off," Jason hisses.

I roll my eyes at him retrieving my knife in the other hand.

I quickly exit the elevator in the direction of the boat shed with purpose in each step. I only make it a few feet before Jason grabs my arm to stop me. I glare up at him.

"The footsteps are in the opposite direction of the boat shed, idiot. We won't make it without a flashlight. Shut up and be quick, so we can go home," I say.

I turn on my heels and continue in the direction I was going. I can hear Jason mumble something behind me, but he falls in step quickly.

The boat shed sits lost in the shadows of the night. None of the lights affixed to its roof are functional. Only the soft glow from the moon illuminates its frame. Making it to the forest edge, I shine my light over the dock. It's empty aside from the chairs and cooler we never cleaned up from earlier. Carefully moving forward, I sweep the light in front of me, looking for any clues.

"Sam," I whisper. "Sam, are you down here?"

I look back at Jason. He nods towards the direction of the building.

Sweeping my light up, we see the door to the shed wide

open. Forgetting all survival instincts, I run into the structure.

"Sam!" I yell. I fling the light in every direction, looking through every corner of the room. The kayaks sit upside down on the ground nearest to the metal garage door that leads to the lake. I fling them over with ease. Nothing.

I turn my attention to the closet in the other corner that holds lake towels, jackets, and various lake toys. I rip each piece out until it's left empty. I turn again, searching for a clue, anything to show where Sam might be.

Jason stands at the entryway watching.

"Don't just stand there, asshole!" I scream. "Sam, where are you?"

Jason doesn't move from his spot.

"She's not here, Ash. We need to keep–"

A scream rips through the darkness behind Jason. Jason flinches before turning to look behind him. I run to meet him at the entrance. With a shaky hand, I raise my light towards the sound. At the start of the dock is a dark lump. It wobbles under the moonlight, standing shakily to its feet. It limps toward us, a whimper cutting through the night. The figure reaches the beam of light twenty-five feet away to reveal its face.

"SAM!"

I bolt from the shed towards her, but my foot catches on something protruding from the ground. I fall face first into the damp earth. My flashlight and knife skitter in front of me, the light still shining towards Sam. A pang racks through my chest. All the air leaves my lungs from the impact. I lay for a second to catch my breath. A dull ache lingers on my right side where my foot made contact with whatever made me lose my footing. Looking up to Sam, my breath catches. Another figure lingers in the distance behind her. It's long strides shortening the distance between them.

"Blood. So much blood. Colton," she chokes out, almost incoherent.

Sam stops. She falters for a second before falling to her knees. She buries her face in her hands as her body shakes from sobs for the loss of our friend.

"Sam. You need to move."

The looming figure is only five steps away now. Close enough for the flashlight to cast light over its mask-covered face. The killer raises an arm to the sky. Their right hand wields an ax, glimmering in the shadows.

Panic rises from inside. Adrenaline masks the pain as I try to untangle myself. Grabbing towards my ankle, I feel the twist of vines and tree roots I tripped over. I rip at the vines fervently to release my leg. I glance back at Sam. The killer is two steps away.

"Sam, RUN!" I scream loosening the last vine from my ankle. Scrambling to my feet, I reach down for my knife and flashlight buried in the dirt, never taking my eyes off of the figure behind Sam.

The killer is one step away.

I'm frozen in place, my subconscious keeping me from helping her.

She looks up to me. Agony etched into her soft features. Her lip trembles as she reaches out a shaky hand towards us, her voice barely a whisper.

"The killer... It's...It's—"

Emerald eyes go sideways as Sam's head falls from her shoulders. A thud echoes into the darkness. Dark liquid sputters from the top of her torso where her head once sat. The body sways before slumping behind the severed head.

A pool of darkness surrounds my friend's lifeless corpse. The killer's figure disappears back into the darkness.

Everything numbs. A scream tears through my throat, hoarse and unyielding. The only thing grounding me in this moment is the tug on my arm. Its force is relentless against my screams. Warm arms wrap around my waist, yanking my eyes from the scene in front of me. Dark eyes fill my vision.

Jason.

He grabs my face between his hands, thumb rubbing against my cheek. His lips move with his voice, but the ringing in my ears almost drowns out his words. My breathing is shallow, leaving me lightheaded.

"Ashe, fucking focus. Can you do that?"

I nod my head automatically. I take a shaky breath to steady myself.

"We're leaving. We just need to grab a cell phone and the keys to the car, then we're leaving. Can you walk?"

I nod again. The pain in my ankle is faint under my crippling spiral.

"But, Sam," I whimper. My lip trembles again.

Jason grabs my shoulders tightly. His dark eyes bore into my own. Sorrow and desperation swirls in their depths, while his face remains stony.

"She's gone. We can't help her or Colton right now. It's just you and me. That's all that matters right now. We can come back for them. I promise."

I scrub my hands down my face, wiping the tears and dirt away. Of course, we can't help them, but we can help ourselves. That's a canon horror movie plot, except this is real life. I know this. We can do this. We can survive.

Taking one shaky final breath, I shake my hands to

release the tension in my body. Get to the cabin. Find a phone. Grab the keys. That's my priority.

"*Fuck* this place," I say with every ounce of confidence I can muster. Gripping my knife tighter, I march past Jason towards the elevator. I can hear him fall in step behind me. The forest is quiet again. A grim reminder of how isolated we are from society. If Jason and I don't make it out, then it could be weeks before anyone realizes we're missing.

Taking mental note, I repeat in my head all the things we need to do in order to survive tonight.

Get to the cabin.

Find a phone and call for help.

Grab the keys.

Leave.

Get to the cabin.

Find a phone and call for help.

Grab the keys.

Leave.

Get to the cabin.

Find a phone and call for help.

Grab the keys.

Leave.

The knife weighs heavy in my hand. Now seeing what the killer is wielding, it feels insignificant in my grasp. I wouldn't have stood a chance against him if I was with Sam this entire time. That thought sits heavy in the back of my mind. I had no way to help her. I wasn't confident enough to handle a gun...

The damn gun.

I stop dead in my tracks. I hear footsteps pad behind me before stopping. My body is tight, ready to defend myself. A knife wouldn't have stopped the killer, but a gun surely would have slowed him down. Tentatively, I turn towards Jason.

He's standing a few feet behind me, his face confused as to why I stopped. I twist the knife in my hand. The blade facing forward for easy slashing. My jaw is clenched under the realization I just had. We sit there staring at each other in silence. The forest humming in the breeze around us.

He's the first to break.

"Why are you staring at me like that? We're almost to the cabin. Keep going."

He motions behind me. I quickly glance in that direction to notice the elevator far off in the corner of the trees before returning my gaze to his. A soft glow of light floats through the darkness. The power must be back on. I take mental note of it while remaining my concentration on Jason.

Anger begins to bubble deep within me.

"Why didn't you help?" I ask.

Jason doesn't move. No change in his demeanor. His body remains relaxed, his face curious.

"What do you mean?"

"Why. Didn't. You. Help?"

"With what, little bat?" he asks, shifting his weight from one foot to the other. His eyes don't leave mine.

I take a step back towards the elevator, ready to run. Something inside me is screaming to run. Something doesn't feel right. *This* doesn't feel right.

"I know you grabbed a gun from the safe, Jason. Why didn't you shoot the killer?"

Jason scoffs at me and takes a step forward. I match his pace with another step back.

"Seriously? You and Sam were both in the way. I wasn't going to put you in danger like that," he says, taking another step forward. Again, I take another step back. I point the knife at him. He holds his hands up and stops advancing.

"Bullshit. Sam died, anyways. You and I both know you're a good shot. You could've bought us time, but you didn't. Why?"

Jason laughs. "Seriously, Ashe. You're losing it. Put the knife down. We have to leave." He steps towards me again, now an arm's length away. I slash the knife at him to create distance and he stumbles back. My steps continue back until my heel hits the door of the elevator.

"Every time something happens, you're not there. Or you conveniently don't help," I say, inching my back along the elevator door to find the edge. I pivot to the side to allow myself space to escape. I will not die because I pinned myself against a wall.

Jason steps forward again, slower than the first time. He says nothing.

"You're working with him, aren't you?"

He freezes. Something wicked flashes in his eyes, gone in an instant, and is replaced by concern. He shakes his head.

"Seriously, Ashe. Did you hit your head when you fell?" he asks. A small laugh fills the air.

"Eat shit, Jason. Answer the damned question," I spit.

He takes another step towards me. "Why would I be working with the killer? What possible advantage does that give me? You guys are my friends. I'm just as gutted as you are that they're dead. But we will be, too, if we don't leave!"

His words are raw and unyielding. The loss of our friends wrapping around every sentence. It would be so convincing if his body language didn't contradict what he said. Tense and ready to pounce, like a predator with their prey. It puts my survival instincts on high alert.

My heart hammers against my chest. It aches at his words. Our friends are dead and the killer is still out here. I didn't ask to be dropped into this horror – one of us did. We just wanted to relive our youth one more time before adulthood took us our separate ways. Now two of us will never see what the future had to offer.

My thoughts are erratic. None of this makes sense. I can't trust anyone. Not Jason. Not the police who came and told us we were being dramatic. Not the public who allowed this maniac to remain free year after year, accepting whatever fate he brought. I'm the only one who can save myself...again.

"Ashe," Jason warns.

"No! Don't *Ashe* me. I can't trust you."

"Ashe, behind you!" Jason runs at me, shoving the knife out of my hand. It scatters somewhere in the distance. He tackles me to the cold ground. Air leaves my lungs for the second time at the impact. His weight is suffocating on top of me. I claw at his back, trying to grip his shirt to help shove him off. My hands slip each time I grip the fabric, now wet. Something warm drips from the sides of Jason's torso onto my chest. Pulling my hands back, I hold them in the moonlight to examine. Blood stains my pale skin. In a panic, I kick my legs against the ground, wiggling just enough to squeeze up Jason's limp body. Once my torso is free, I sit up. An ax is buried into Jason's back, the blood trickling in all directions from the wound.

Half lucid, Jason looks up at me. "Run," he whispers before falling unconscious. Behind him lingers the shadow of my past. The ghostly reminder that no one is safe from being hunted.

SIXTEEN

The night blurs around me in slow motion. Sounds ricochet through my skull. The damp, coldness of the night chills me to the bone. My feet stumble to connect with the ground beneath me. Hands dig into the earth to propel me forward towards the cabin. Dirt sticks to every surface covered in my friends' blood. Earthly smells begin mixing with the coppery tang I will never be able to forget.

The dark presence remains in the distance. Death personified on silent steps, waiting. I rush towards the elevator, flinging the door open with a slam. I frantically smash the *up* button, willing it to move faster than the gears will allow. I check over my shoulder to track the figure in the distance.

Empty.

The forest is empty.

"Shit, shit, shit," I whimper, pacing around the elevator car in a panic.

I'm completely open on this damned contraption. I curse myself for not running up the hill towards the front door. Quickly scanning my surroundings as I ascend, I press my back flat against the back of the elevator. The machine chugs along towards the deck. Gears click into the forest in front of me like a death clock.

Rising into the treetops, I change position to face the deck floor, hands gripping the edge as my only anchor to sanity. Inch by inch, the deck comes into view. Flood lights illuminating the sky. It's not until the elevator comes to a full stop that I let out the breath I didn't know I was holding. No foreboding presence is awaiting my arrival.

Carefully, I unlatch the door, scanning my surroundings to ensure I don't get ambushed. After a beat of silence, I break into a full sprint into the cabin, careful to avoid the remnants of Colton's body scattered across the ground. A mantra for survival repeating in my head.

Cell phone.

Keys.

Car.

Survive.

I trip over the metal coffee table in the middle of the room as I round its corners towards the front door. The sharp corner gouges into my shin, making my wince. A warm, radiating sensation tingles up my leg. I shove down my need to stop and check the wound. A little cut is the least of my worries right now.

I let out a sigh of relief as the entryway comes into view. All our cellphones are neatly placed where I had last left them. Sliding to a stop in front of the table near the front door, I fumble to grab my phone. Nothing happens when I click the side button to wake it. I click again, but the black screen stares back at me. The darkness reflects the grim night ahead of me. I throw my phone down and grab another. Then another. All our phones are dead. All phones except for Jason's. Fingers tremble as I try to enter his pass-code. The screen flashes at me.

Incorrect Pass Code.

"What?!" I shriek into the void of the cabin.

We've always shared pass codes in case of emergencies. *Always* told the group if we had to update the pass codes. Jason's had the same one since high school. Or so I thought. I don't know what to think about him anymore. *Thought* about him. Because he fell, too. He's dead, too.

Something deep inside tugs at that thought. Sadness ripples through me and I squeeze my eyes shut. Tears threaten to spill over. Shakily, I take three deep breaths. There will be a time and a place to mourn what I lost today, but not now.

With the final breath, I open my eyes. Staring down at the phone screen, I swipe at the *emergency* button. Relief floods through me as a number keypad appears. Quickly, I tap 911.

Glass shatters around me before my thumb hits *call*. A scream escapes me as I raise my arms to shield my face. I stumble away from the glittery, violent shards falling in the air as I back into the love seat in the living room. Removing my arms and looking in front of me, dark eyes stare back at me behind a bloodied mask in the hole of the glass panel.

"Leave me alone!" I demand.

The eyes disappear, replaced by an arm that reaches through the opening for the deadbolt.

"No!"

I race forward and, with all my strength, slam my fists

into that dark arm. It swings back at me, grabbing my neck before shoving me back. Returning to the door, the killer's hand finds the deadbolt lock and flicks it open. The arm retreats from the hole in the glass panel into the darkness.

My body is frozen in place in the entryway. My breath is uneven as I stare into that blackened emptiness next to the front door. Blood pounds in my ears, drowning out everything around me. Images race through my mind as I try to collect myself with what I should do next.

Breaking my thoughts, the front door swings open, banging into the wall behind it. I jump at the sound and look into the night beyond the entrance. Painted on a skull mask, staring back at me on a hulking frame, are those three bloody words:

Time to play

"Absolutely fucking not," I mutter. I will my body to run. I sprint to the kitchen towards the knife block. An empty knife block. I search the counter and the drawers closest to me. Everything is gone.

How is that even possible?!

Heavy footsteps pull me from my panic. Ditching the offer of defense, I rip the backdoor open and run into the darkness. The full moon hides behind the clouds again, my only light dims from the overcast of the deck floodlights. I run my way to the perimeter of the cabin. Somewhere out here is the small work shed that houses the gardening tools and circuit breaker. At least, that's how Colton made it sound. I prayed to the gods my hunch was right.

As I round the far corner, nearest to our bedrooms, a small wooden structure appears. I skitter to a stop a few feet away. Eyes and ears straining, I search for any whisper of the killer's approach. I inch towards the shack, careful of each step, as if I could muffle the sound of sticks and leaves breaking under foot if I went slower. Swinging the latch open, an automated light flicks to life overhead.

Various garden tools lay about the walls, none of them in an organized fashion. I glance behind me before sifting through the mess in front of me. I'm looking for something suitable enough to stab with when I spot the circuit breaker on the back wall behind a large shovel. Pushing the spade out of the way, a gasp escapes my lips. A rainbow of wires hang out of the belly of the breaker box. The longest of them, a red one, is crudely twisted together in the middle. Following the wire back to the box, I spy the label the wire is connected to.

Main Cabin

"You've got to be shitting me."

My fingers play with the bundle in my hand, careful not to touch the exposed wires.

That explains why the power went out earlier. It wasn't from the storm, it was intentional. The killer has been here the whole time. They had this planned. They knew we'd be up here this weekend. Which means they've either been stalking us or someone made a deal with the devil.

I drop the electrical cord to survey my surroundings. The tiny shed is filled to the brim with gardening equipment. I only assume the equipment was used by Colton and his brother to keep the grounds clean, as part of their bargain to use this cabin without complaint from Mommy and Daddy dearest. My skin prickles at the damp chill wafting in from the open door. I wrap my arms around myself and rub my hands over the goosebumps forming on my exposed skin. Eyes wandering, they fall on a metal-tipped pickax in the corner. Shoving the supplies out of the way, I pull it from its resting place. The smooth grain of the wood is cool against my touch. The weight of the tool is hefty in my grip, but it's doable. I could easily gouge an eye out or rip a shoulder blade *My Bloody Valentine* style, if needed.

Leaves crackle in the distance behind me. My head whips around to the open door. My body is rigid as I stare back into the forest beyond me. Waiting a few beats, I tiptoe to the entrance. Placing both hands against the door, I ease it closed slowly, leaving just enough space so it doesn't latch against the door jam. A sliver of clouded moonlight peeks in through the opening. I turn to lean my back against the door, hand remaining on the inside handle.

My breathing picks up, shallow and rapid. I twist the handle of the pickax in my hand, trying to disperse the sweat from my palm. Closing my eyes, I inhale deeply, willing my body to calm. Flashes of a cool, fall night rush against my eyelids. Scenes of blood, metal, and dirt come flooding back. I'm wrought with emotions as I remember that fateful night. I killed that night for survival. I could do it again. I will do it again.

With a renewed sense of purpose, I take another deep breath and peer out of the door frame. The killer's massive shadow lurks just past the edge of the shed. I strain my ears to listen. Leaves crunch softly close by. I grip the pick handle tighter and lean against the door, ready to strike. I soften my breathing so I don't give away my hiding spot too early.

The killer thuds by slowly. Masked eyes scanning the landscape in front of them. I lean forward to try and get a better look, but the door creaks against my weight. That bloodied face whips in my direction. I flinch back, closing my eyes and praying to the gods they don't investigate. I hear a few steps towards my hiding spot. A long pause that feels like an eternity. Then the killer turns back to their path, walking right past the shed door. I look out again, gearing up for my attack.

Once the killer is several feet away, I push the door open quietly. Placing both hands on the handle, I raise the pickax with a vicious grip. Eyes narrow in on their right shoulder where the killer holds their own tool of death. Closing the gap between us, I slam the pointed end of the pick down. A scream tears from my throat as the metal finds its home in the meaty center of their shoulder. A muffled gasp escapes from the masked figure. I rip the metal tip out and shove with all my strength into the killer's back. They stumble forward into the dampen ground, dropping their own ax in the process. They whip a hand out at me and I dodge it, jumping towards where the square blade lays on the ground. I bend to pick up the ax, not taking my eyes off of my tormentor.

"You killed them," I growl.

I firmly grip the ax handle and stand.

"We're not even in high school anymore. We don't fit in your game. Yet you still killed them," I cry out, taking two steps towards the wounded animal still kneeling on the ground. One hand holds the injured shoulder and I can hear a labored breathing behind the mask. Blank eyes stare up at me.

"You weren't even merciful. And now I'm going to carve you into pieces!"

Before the killer can stand back up, I slash the ax down on their other shoulder. Their deep cry fills the night sky. I kick them in the chest to dislodge the ax as they fall to the ground. Like a rabid animal, I jump over top of them and bring the ax down again into their midsection. Warm blood splatters from the impact, mixing with the dried blood already on my hands. I yank the ax up again and bring it back down, this time into the killer's chest. They wheeze at the impact. Blood spurts out again as a cracking noise fills the chilled air.

Sitting my full weight on top of them, I repeat this process. Over and over again, beating their rib cage with the blade of the ax. Each time going deeper into their chest cavity. Their arms shiver at their side, limp and inoperable from the ripped tendons in each shoulder socket. Everything turns red as I unleash all my pent up rage. All the pain and gut wrenching sadness from the loss of my friends. All the years seniors were picked off one by one for their sick and twisted games. I slash with every emotion in me until the life below me ceases to exist.

TIME TO DIE

SEVENTEEN

Air scratches my throat like broken glass as I suck in a deep breath. My hands tremble in front of me, still holding the ax in a vice grip. The smell of wet dirt, copper, and sour bile invades my nostrils. Dropping the tool, I hold back a gag with my hands. My palms are sticky and the scent of blood is everywhere. I'm covered in it. I try to even my breathing by inhaling through my nose.

"Rest in pieces, shit bag," I hiss to myself. I shake my hands a few times, attempting to will myself to calm down. I crack my knuckles together and take inventory of my body.

No major limbs missing. No broken bones. Any exposed skin is cut to shit from running through the trees. My right ankle throbs in protest under my body's weight, but I can still use it.

Finally able to take a second to process the events that

just occurred, I stare down at the lifeless body in front of me. It's massive. Like the size of a football player. Like…

Colton.

No fucking way.

There's only one other person in town who shares the same body composition as Colton.

I fling the ax to the side. Getting off the body and kneeling down, I move a shaky hand towards the body in front of me. It flinches and an arm jolts into the air. I jump back at the movement. A shrill yelp reverberates through the night. I pause for a few seconds before gently placing my fingers at the corpse's carotid.

No pulse.

I let out a hallowed breath. It's just a death rattle. A really severe one, but the person is dead, nonetheless.

Returning my hand to the body's face, I remove the soiled hockey mask. Glossy, vacant eyes stare up at me. The jaw is slack and sunken back into the skull, skin waxen under the moon's glow. It's not the killer, but one of their loyal servants. Even in this state of rigor and brutal abuse, I know exactly who's been torturing us.

"You cocky son of a bitch. How did you get tricked into this," I ask, mentally condemning Tyler from the grave.

I sit back onto the damp earth, the icy wetness pricking through my shorts into my skin. Bringing my legs towards me, I hang my head between my thighs. I take deep breaths in an attempt to process all the events of tonight. I really thought The Slayer was back. How would anyone would have known *Tyler,* Colton's brother, of all people, was the one tormenting us? Stalking us. Killing us.

Oh, gods.

He killed Colton, his own brother. He killed Sam. He killed Jason.

A ragged cry racks my body. I slump down and sink into hopelessness. Sobbing for everything I've lost and everything I'll never be able to experience. I'm forever alone in this shit show of reality. No one will believe me when I tell them what occurred here. My mind races a million miles a minute behind the heavy tears to make sense of the carnage. Nothing adds up.

We found the mask at the lake– I know for a fact that was real. The notes we found seemed too sophisticated. Too intentional. How I found my friends is too near perfect to how The Senior Slayer conducted his spree years ago. Yet, it's outside of hunting season for his games and Tyler doesn't have a motive. His family is extremely well off. He doesn't have to kill for money. So, what am I missing?

Snap.

My head whips up at the sound of branches breaking in the distance. I cup my mouth with both hands to attempt to muffle my cries. I stare towards the right where I heard the sound come from.

Snap.

I jump back with a whimper. The sound now drifts from the left of me. I try scanning into the moonlit forest, but my eyes struggle to make out anything against the trees.

"Hello," I whisper.

Silence descends the seconds after my question.

"I-is anyone there? Help. I need help!" I say louder.

Snap.

The sound is now directly behind me. I freeze, shrinking as if I could conceal myself among the leaves. Nails dig into the dirt in a futile attempt to ground myself. The hairs on the back of my neck stand on edge while my nerves tingle just beneath my skin. Adrenaline surges through my body again. The only thing I can hear is the blood pulsating against my ear drums. I hold my breath as I turn my head to look over my shoulder.

I let out a breath when I see glowing eyes above my head. I realize it's just an owl in rustling through the trees. But then the trees start moving. Their shadows become bigger as they come closer. I'm stuck to the ground, unable to move as I stare at the darkness coming towards me. My brain is screaming at me to start moving. It isn't until the shadowy blur turns into a shadowy figure stalking towards me. I will my legs to push me up. I start running, well, hobbling, as quickly as I can to put distance between us.

"Leave me alone!" I scream. I pray to the universe this is just a figment of my imagination. A hallucination from pure exhaustion. I look back to check my surroundings and watch as the shadow picks up the discarded pickax I had moments earlier.

Final girl rule 101: don't lose your weapon. How did I forget that?!

Twisting through the trees, I can make out the silhouette of the cabin ahead. If I can make it to the deck, I can find Jason's cellphone to call for help. My lungs ache as I struggle through each breath. Despite the pain, I will myself to keep moving forward. Help is only a few feet away. My ankle stings in protest from the overexertion. I shove down my pain as best as I can. Survival is the only thing I need to worry about right now.

The soft earth turns to solid concrete. I know I'm close to the cabin's front door. I wave my hands in the air in an attempt to activate the motion sensor flood lights on the front stoop. A few more steps and I'm blinded by white. Light illuminates the scene in front of me as I enter the cabin. Colton's corpse remains a statue on the bloodied couch. The low hum of bugs invading their new home whispers into the room. The stale air mixing with the grizzly scene makes my gag reflex return with a cruel vengeance. Holding my breath, I scan the floor looking for the phone I dropped earlier.

Black glitter shines back at me under the foot of the love seat against the littering of broken glass. Walking over, I quickly locate the phone. Spider web cracks cover the screen. I flick my thumb up the center, praying it still works. I let out a sigh of relief when the lock screen appears. Somehow, cell service has returned to normal. Through shaky hands, I tap the phone app and dial 911. It only takes one ring before someone picks up.

"911. What is your emergency," a gentle voice asks from the other end.

"Help! My name is Ashe Nikko. Please. All my friends are dead. The Senior Slayer, I think they're here. We're at the James Family cabin, off of Lake Hill Road. Oh my god, they're all dead," I cry into the phone. Trembles overcome my body.

"Okay, miss. Remain calm. You said The Slayer? Murdered your friends? How much have you had to drink tonight?" dispatch asks.

"What?! Did you not hear me? I said there are DEAD BODIES. I'm not fucking drunk," I scream at the dispatcher.

Clicks from a keyboard float through the receiver. I can hear mumbling in the background.

"Okay, miss. And you haven't taken any illegal substances tonight?" dispatch asks.

"No," I huff. I spin on my heels in a circle, trying to scan my surroundings. The figure following me hasn't emerged from the forest.

Yet.

"Look. I'm completely sober. I know this sounds ridiculous, but you need to send people here now," I grind out.

More ticks of the keyboard fill the line. It feels like a whole minute goes by before dispatch responds.

"Miss, we can have officers out within the hour. The storm blocked a lot of critical roads leading to your current location," dispatch reports.

I take a steadying breath.

"I don't have an hour! The killer is still. Out. Here."

"I will notify the officers this is priority, level one, miss," dispatch offers. "I need you to stay on the phone with me until they arrive."

Light dims behind me. I turn to become face-to-face with the damned skull mask. It's deadly warning etched into the forehead.

"Miss," dispatch prompts. "Are you still there?"

"They're here," I whisper. I begin backing up onto the back deck.

"Who is? Can you provide a name."

My back makes contact with the door of the elevator as I look around for an escape. The figure stands at the edge of the deck, blocking any sort of exit through the cabin or back through the woods. The only way out is down.

"Fucking hell," I curse to myself. "The killer is still here. Send help now!"

I shove the phone in my pocket. The figure is walking towards me, picking up the pace with each step. Frantic, I fumble with the key to turn the elevator on. Looking up again, the figure is at the entrance of the elevator. I slam the lever and the elevator shoots down just before the figure can throw the ax towards my head.

TIME TO DIE

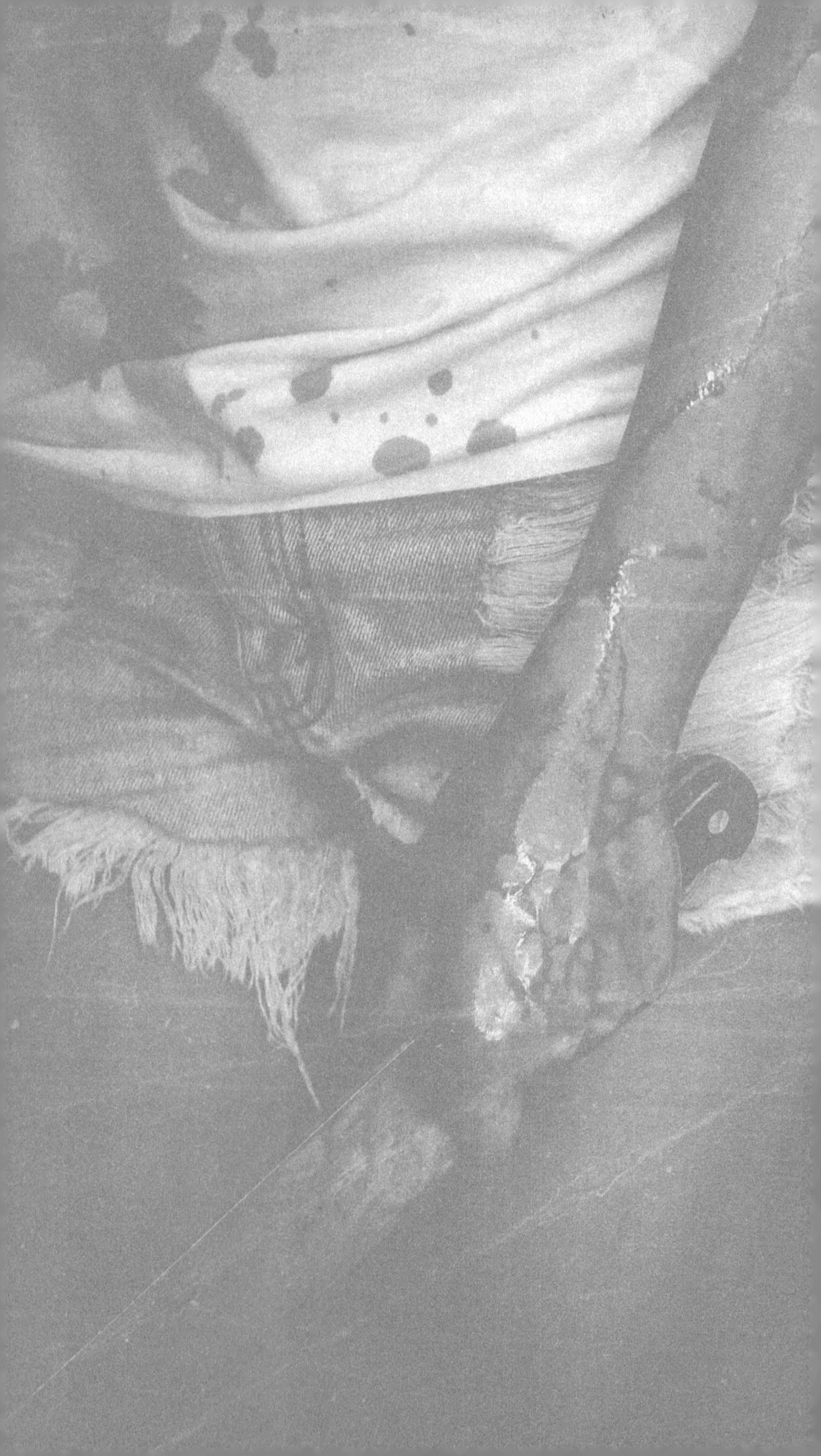

EIGHTEEN

The elevator slams into the ground and I fling the door open as it clatters against the steel foundation. I push my feet forward with the remaining strength I have left. Branches scratch against every inch of exposed flesh as I weave through the trees. Each cut is a reminder of my impending doom.

Silent sobs consume my body. My mouth is dry and my throat burns with each haggard breath. I keep moving forward, I cannot allow myself to stop now. I thought I was so close to being free. I stumble through the thicket of greenery into a clearing. My eyes blink to bring everything into view.

The lake shed glows ahead, all of its twinkling lights now illuminating the wooden dock. Pushing myself forward, I run towards the door as my trembling hands grasp the door knob. I try to push the door open, knob twisting, but the door remains closed.

"Come on. I don't have time for this," I cry. "Please, please, please open."

I jiggle the knob and shove my weight against the door. Once. Twice. On the third time, the door swings open. I scramble inside and slam the door close behind me. I press my back against the hard surface and lean my head back. The tears I was holding back return with a vengeance. Warm liquid leaks down my face as my chest heaves with a heaviness. I can't do this. Not by myself. I don't want to.

I can't do this.

I can't do this.

I can't do this.

Each word is a tear at my broken soul. Everyone thinks they want to be the final girl, but no one talks about the cost of becoming one. Final girl means you are the last one standing. Final girl means everyone you loved has died. Final girl means you are alone.

I barely have time to collect myself when piercing, hot pain cuts through my mental fog. I scream out and try to jerk my right leg away from the pain. It doesn't move. Looking down, the gleaming, red tip of the pickax protrudes from the door. Its rounded tip rests deep into my calf, blood spilling from the opening. I try to yank my leg away again, wincing at the effort. Suddenly, the weapon is ripped from the opening. I cry out and fall to the floor as the searing pain shoots through me. Flipping on my backside, I try dragging myself upward against the shelves behind me. My leg buckles under the weight. Rolling over again, I begin crawling towards the garage door that leads directly to the water.

I can hear the crack of the door swinging open behind

me. Rage replaces the fear in my heart. Sending a silent prayer of courage to whomever will listen, I turn over and stare my attacker down. Their body fills the doorway. The masked figure tips their head to one side as dark eyes glare at me. Somewhere in my subconscious, I recognize those familiar eyes.

I bare my teeth as I continue to scramble my way backwards.

"You're fucking disgusting. I bet your micro peen is so hard for this right now." The words leave my mouth before I have time to think of the consequences.

I watch as the killer stalks closer to me, watching me through the skull mask they wear. Black, haunted eyes stare back at me. The pickax they used to mutilate my leg scrapes behind them, sparking over the concrete floor of the cabin shed.

Shit.

Of course, my smart ass would have some sarcastic quip before I die.

The killer isn't even phased by my remark. It'd be kind of a turn on to be chased by a masked man if I wasn't about to die.

I painstakingly crawl my way to the back door, my mutilated leg dragging behind me. Stained, red meat tendrils protrude from my thigh while blood gushes from the open orifice. The dribbles of blood smeared beneath my leg taunts the killer towards me like fishing chum in the water. My weakening body asks the killer to take hold and yank me back to my death. Each breath is ragged.

Fuck. Fuck. FUCK.

There's only ten feet between possible freedom and the most horrific death I could ever imagine for myself. Who would've thought this would be how I would go out.

My friends would be cheering me on...if they were still here.

Each inch feels like miles through shards of glass. The excruciating pain radiates from my mangled limb, racking my body with shivers. It makes it nearly impossible to move forward. I'm going to go into shock before I make it out of here.

"Please. I'm sorry," I choke out. "Help me!". The words don't hold the sincerity I want them to, rage still lingers in my voice. It doesn't waver, my words too strong in their conviction. I'm staring down my hunter with hatred and primal fear.

Maybe I can convince the killer to have mercy. If only for a second, I could have a chance. I could make it out. I could save my leg and survive a little longer.

And then I can hunt this motherfucker down and hang them with their own intestines while they watch me feed their severed cock to the wildlife.

The killer stands over me, the pickax hung low by their side. Hollow eyes stare at me through the bloodied mask. They turn their head to one side and the other. Another familiar movement that clicks somewhere deep within my mind. Contemplating me with whatever sick fetish they have. The smell of blood, dirt, and sweat fills the space. The air is heavy between us. I'm entranced in their gaze. My deadly fate, only inches from me.

A low, masculine chuckle emanates from the angel of death above me. The killer kneels down and pulls me up by the throat. I yelp in surprise, whimpering under their tight hold that would in any other situation make me dripping wet. Their right knee pins my good leg to the ground while their left knee tucks between my legs, digging into my crotch. The pain I was feeling escalates to one hundred. The killer pulls me close enough I can feel their damp breath on my face. Blood crusted fingers tighten around my neck, making it harder to breathe before they finally speak.

"Micro peen, huh? That's not what you were saying earlier when I was deep inside of you, making you cum all over my cock. Now be a good girl and shut the fuck up, Ashe. It's time to die." The voice is deep and guttural. I stare in horror as the killer slides the bloodied mask over their face to rest on top of dark hair.

The familiar face above me smiles.

My blood curdles.

Time stands still. I can't move my eyes from theirs. The amber pools that I found my release in just a few hours ago are black. They stare down at me with indifference. The moment we shared earlier is gone, replaced by a murderous haze.

The room begins spinning. My vision starts to blur. Black spots cover every inch of the room. I'm spiraling into oblivion. My mental state can't take the scene unfolding in front of me. How poetic— the murder obsessed author goes out at the hands of their lover who turns out to be a serial killer.

The inside of my mind feels like a deep trance. I'm grasping at the killer's strong arms, trying to anchor myself to reality.

It's not my time yet. I won't go. I can't. I refuse to go down without a fight.

I choke out one last word before darkness takes me over.

"Jason."

NINETEEN

"I *t's time to wake up, Ashe.*"

The voice is muffled, lost in a distant fog. I can't pull myself back to reality. I'm floating in my nightmares, running from an imaginary killer.

The heat of an object making contact with my cheek raises me from my unconscious state. Footsteps disappear into the distance.

"Wake the fuck up, Ashe. It's time to play."

My eyes flutter open, they strain against the light above me. *Where the fuck am I?* I try to move my body to sit up, but I can't. My arms and legs are tied back. A hot sting radiates from my right side.

My leg. I almost died! I should be dead. Why the hell am I not dead right now?

I'm thrashing against my restraints. It's the same red rope Jason brought at the beginning of the trip.

Jason.

My whole body is stuck in place. Metal digs into my

skin as I fight against the restraints. I'm very aware that my clothes are missing from the chill that hovers over my exposed breasts. My eyes begin to focus.

I'm in the cabin tied to the coffee table in the living room.

The lights are glaring overhead. I turn my head to shield from the unusually bright light. I'm faced with the discarded body of my dead friend slumped over the couch. A puddle of blood pooled underneath the feet of the soiled furniture. Tears well behind my eyes as I stare at the scene of what my horrific future will hold.

A shuffle in the corner grabs my attention.

I look over. Jason is sitting in one of the chairs at the window.

"There she is. Welcome back to the living, little bat. How kind of you to finally join us."

I stare blankly.

Dead. He's supposed to be dead.

"I watched you die. You had an ax to your back. You were bleeding. You told me to *run!*"

Jason laughs, low and deep. It sends shivers down my spine. Slowly, rising from the chair, he saunters over to where I'm held captive in the center of the room. His midnight amber eyes are on mine the entire time, a burning desire behind them. To kill or to fuck, I can't be sure.

"I did in fact have an ax in my back and I was bleeding. Good job. What an astute observation you've made, captain." Jason grabs the hem of his sweatshirt and pulls it over his head, discarding it on the floor. Strapped to his body is a tan vest with Velcro attached to his chest over both shoulders. He does a spin for me, like a model at a fashion show. The back of the vest reveals a splattering of red accompanied by a deep gash between his shoulder blades.

"Nothing a little Kevlar, duct tape, and a bag of watered down ketchup can't fake."

I gape at him in disbelief. "Where did you find that?"

Jason twirls like a ballerina, showing off the ripped vest.

"Oh, this dusty, old thing? Found it in the safe while I was grabbing weapons. Turns out, it came in handy since Tyler was ready to kill my ass along with you guys."

"FUCK. YOU. Jason. Rot in hell!"

I try moving as far away as I can in my captive state. My brain clicks back into survival mode. *I'm not doing this again. I was supposed to be safe!* It's obviously useless. I'm locked in place. Even if I could escape, I can barely walk, let alone run.

Jason takes his time reaching me, his large, muscular frame outlined by the shadows behind him. A demon stalking his soul to claim. He drags out each step, assessing me with hungry desire. The sounds of Velcro releasing fills the space as he removes the vest. Reaching where I lay helpless, he traces the outline of my body on the table. His long, bloodstained index finger drags along the smooth table. My skin prickles with anticipation. He's so close to touching me, yet so far away all at once. He's watching my body react with each movement of his hand. I try to clamp my legs closed to avoid him touching my most sensitive parts. The muscles in his jaw feather before a smirk outlines his face. He's enjoying this game.

Disgusting. I knew he was a kinky asshole, I didn't know he was a demented masochist. Even I draw the line at snuff films to get off and yet he's doing this live, in person. It makes my stomach roll. Bile rises in my throat. I swallow it down with my naivety, thinking my past wouldn't come back to haunt me.

"Jason, let me go. I need medical attention. My leg. I'm going to bleed out," I plead.

Jason doesn't take his eyes off of where his finger is tracing on the table. He shrugs. The smirk disappears from his chiseled features. It's replaced with a look of indifference, like he's thinking of how to answer. He continues to trace around my body, careful to not touch me. Silence spreads between us— it's unsettling. My breath hitches each time I feel his heated touch graze against my skin. I'm on fire, waiting for him to touch me or kill me. I don't care whichever, just put me out of this misery.

Jason sighs and takes a step back after what seems like an eternity. He squares his shoulders and shakes his head, clearing his mind.

"You won't. At least not now. I pulled a Jigsaw and cauterized your leg when you were passed out. No major veins were hit. You're patched up long enough for me to have my fun."

"A Jigsaw?" I ask, confusion lacing my words.

"Come on, Ashe," he drawls, dragging out my name like we're suddenly best friends again. "Jigsaw. The *Saw* movies? *Saw 1*'s escape? They cauterize the leg on a heated water pipe. Even you should know that reference."

I somehow find the energy to scoff at him. "That wasn't Jigsaw who lost their leg, idiot. That was Lawrence and it was just his foot."

Jason shrugs nonchalantly, "Then consider yourself lucky you still have everything intact."

"Oh, yeah. *So* lucky that you spared my life instead of brutally murdering me like Sam and Colton," I snide at him.

"I should be so grateful that my captor saved my life. However should I repay you?"

Jason locks eyes with mine. Darkness burns in their golden depths. I try my damnedest to plead with my eyes to release me.

I thought we were friends, Jason. Please, let me go.

"You could choke on my cock until you stop breathing," he sneers.

"I should've never fucked you! You're nothing but a selfish, demented cunt. Your dick isn't even that good of a lay." I'm screaming at him, thrashing against the table. The metal bites into my bare skin. If he won't let me go, then I'm fighting to the death.

"One: We both know damn well that's a lie, Ashe. You loved having my thick cock split you in half. Two: Cunt is a little extreme and unbecoming of a lady." Jason turns away from me, rummaging on the couch just out of sight.

"FUCK. YOU. JASON." I yell each word with conviction.

"And, three," He turns back to me, a familiar knife in hand. "As you wish. Just remember you asked for this."

He stalks back towards me wielding the glimmering blade I used hours earlier on him. The veins in his hand pop as he tightens his grip around the handle. I watch as he plays with the knife in his hands. The swirls of black ink on his forearms dance with each flex of muscle as he twists it this way and that.

"Wh-what are you going to do with that?" I stutter, my eyes wide as I watch him cautiously.

He places the sharp end tentatively against the exposed skin on my inner thigh. I stiffen in response, knowing damn well with one well-placed gash, he could bleed me out in minutes.

The cold blade trails up and down my leg. I shiver.

Goosebumps raise on the spot the blade teases. I'm trying my hardest to stay still. I can feel my core warm to the touch. My body, used to knife play with my previous partners, betrays my rational mind. A moan escapes my lips before I realize what's happening.

Jason smiles. He knows this is my weakness. He's entranced by the blade against my skin as he talks. Inch by inch, the knife gets closer to my aroused core.

"The Senior Slayer - *Master* - has something special planned for you. You think you can take his stories and profit from them? Live your own life and not follow The Order? You think you're better than us because you channel your inner demons into your books? You walk around like horror and smut make your world go round. Well, little bat, let's see how much you like it when you are the main character."

A plea tears through me before I have a chance to think.

"Slayer! Slayer, slayer, slayer!"

A sinister laugh echoes through the empty cabin.

"Your safe word won't help you anymore."

TIME TO DIE

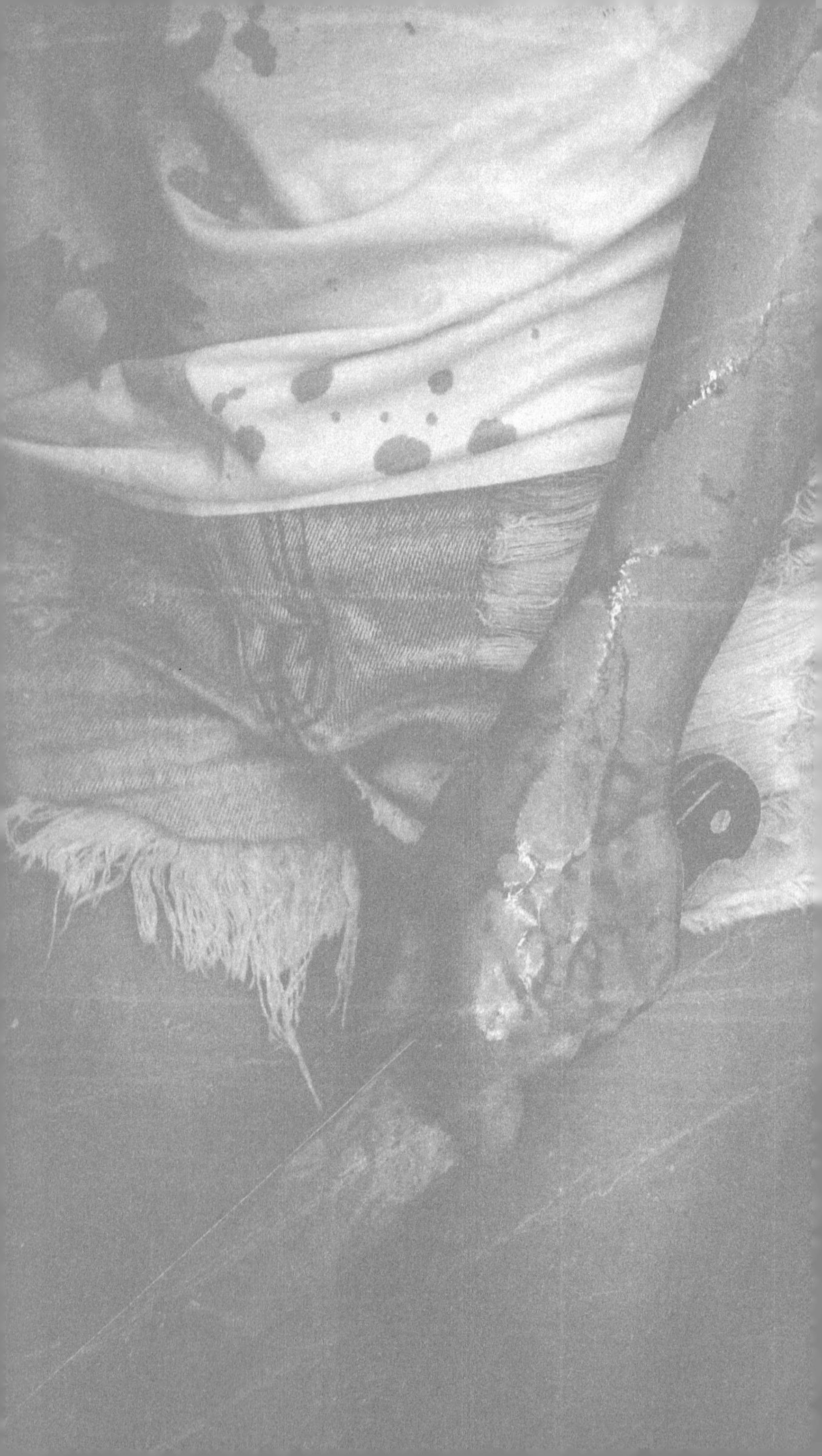

TWENTY

Screams bounce off the living room walls. It takes a minute to register that the sound is coming from me. I watch, hopelessly pulling to try and get free, as Jason jerks the blade of the knife upward between my legs. Searing, hot pain radiates from my center. I slam my head down against the hard table. The motion reverberates through my skull, dazing my consciousness. Wetness envelopes the spot where the blade made contact. Sticky as glue, the puddle becomes larger underneath my exposed ass.

Shivers rack my body, my skin hyper sensitive to every sensation as I lay prone on the freezing table. I continue to thrash against the restraints. The rope around my left wrist slips. It's slight, but there's no denying the tug I felt. I glare at Jason as he stalks around me, holding his attention as I continue to wriggle my wrist against the restraint. His knife drags across the table top, screeching with each step.

"If you're going to kill me, do it. Stop fucking around," I bark, baring my teeth at him.

His fingers float onto my face, caressing my jaw line. I snap my teeth towards his unwelcome touch. Jason flinches, pulling back an inch. With the speed of a viper, he cracks his palm across cheek. I gasp for air. My back arches in response to the pain before I right myself on the table. I shoot him a withering look, wishing I could melt him with my stare.

Holding the knife to my neck, Jason leans in. "There's no fun in cold meat. Besides, aren't you going to ask me how I did it? Any good final girl would, baby." He croons each word like a lullaby as he slowly slices the blade at the backside of my neck. My jaw clenches against the sensation and I swallow down the pain.

Jason stalks lower on my body, his eyes wandering over my naked frame. He's drinking in every piece of me, stripping bare beneath his gaze before he cuts again. This time, the blade grazes the center of my stomach. I lurch forward in the restraints at the contact, careful not to pull too hard on my left side.

Jason raises his gaze back to mine, lust filling those hollow, dull irises. His lips are parted slightly as his breathing shallows. Grime-covered fingers slip through the fresh wound on my abdomen, digging deeper as I cry out. It feels like he's ripping me open from the inside out. Those fingers, bloodied and slick, slide down. Down. Down. Resting at my entrance, Jason gingerly rubs his thumb across my clit. Mentally, I flinch back from his touch, but my body betrays me. Leaning into his touch, Jason grins. Callus fingers play with swollen folds as his thumbs continues its relentless rhythm.

"You want this. Just admit it. You're depraved and twisted, just like me."

"No," I growl.

"There's a little killer in there, isn't there? And she wasn't created tonight. No, no." He chuckles. "The little killer has been there all along. Living under the surface, begging to be let out to play."

I jerk my face away from his, choking against the foul smell emanating from his blood soaked clothes.

"I'm nothing like you."

"Oh, but you are. Or did you not kill Tristan our senior year to be saved from becoming The Slayer's next victim?"

My eyes widen.

No one knows about that. They can't. I never told anyone.

"Ah. You don't know. You took that check he gave you and never tried contacting him, hm? Well, let me be the first to tell you— congratulations. You found the one loophole in Master's game. He doesn't like that too much, no." He chuckles to himself. "No, he doesn't. Not one bit. So, over the past year, Master has been..." he pauses, mulling over what word to say next, "recruiting people for a new kind of game.

"You are his greatest achievement. And his greatest failure. No one knows why Master plays his games. Why he picks the victims he does, but it all serves a purpose." Jason walks away, hands open towards the sky. "It's all meticulously planned for a bigger picture only he knows. So," he quips, with a little bounce in his step back towards me, "since you inadvertently broke the rules of the game, he changed it. Anyone who has graduated from Graveslake High after his original killing spree is eligible. Instead of recruiting one person to do his bidding, he made a public declaration for open season on you. One just had to know where to look. A random post on the dark corner of the internet most people don't visit."

I don't say anything as I stare at him. My lips pull into a tight line as I focus on my wrist, the restraint becoming looser with each movement. Jason pauses for a second before continuing his stalk around my pinned body, the dull knife leaving its torturous scrape against my tender flesh.

"Tyler found the post first, fucking around on the dark web, searching for porn. The idiot. He thought it was a prank. He sent it to me asking to verify it, since Ty didn't want big bro to know and I was crazy enough to attempt contact." Jason shrugs. "You can use your big author brain to imagine our surprise when *he* responded to us with *his* proposal."

"So, what? You guys decided to go halfsies on killing me? How romantic. It's like a match made in heaven."

Jason flicks the tip of the knife across my forearm. I wince at the burn, groaning under my breath. "Something like that." He crosses to the other side of me and flicks the knife again, the tip digging into the skin just below my elbow.

"We were warned that you were different. That you had *killed*. We had to be careful on how we completed our task. To earn our prize."

Jason returns to my face. I turn my head in a futile attempt to get away. He grabs my neck, pulling me upward. The knife settles at the base of my throat and I yelp. It takes everything in me to keep my bottom lip from trembling.

"Tyler didn't want in, at first. Being the golden boy and all. It wasn't too hard to convince him. That pay out would still be more than he would inherit from his parents. He found out last year they changed their will to donate half of their inheritance to some backwoods charity when they kick the bucket. Poor little rich boy didn't like his retirement being sold out from under him, so he agreed in order to get the money he so desperately desired."

He inclines my face towards his until our lips nearly touch. The heat from his lips flutter over my own. I still at the contact before attempting to shake my head to get him off me. His grip on my neck tightens.

"All we needed to do was bring your severed head to the drop point and all the spoils would be ours. Well, mine. Good job taking care of Tyler, by the way."

I stop fighting his merciless hold and remain silent at Jason's comment. He continues without pause.

"I planned on taking him out at some point to tie up loose ends and keep the money all for myself. I didn't realize he planned on mimicking The Slayer's original killings to the letter. Who would've known he was secretly a corpse fucker? And his own brother of all people! Revolting little cunt."

His hand slithers its way to my warm center, fingers grazing between my slick folds. My body arches on instinct and I whimper at the unwanted contact. A tear slips from my cheek. "I prefer my meat more," he pauses as he watches my body react, "warm and tender."

His fingers slip inside and I cry out, straining against the restraints.

"No!"

He pumps his finger deeper. A second finger circling my clenched backside.

"Oh, yes, sweetheart." The second finger presses through my tight muscles, matching the punishing speed. My body convulses at the intrusion as tears begin spilling down my face.

Jason continues his relentless assault on me, eyeing my body's response.

"I had half a mind to kill Tyler myself. However, he caught me off guard, starting our game earlier than expected, so I never got the chance."

Without warning, he removes his fingers from me. The emptiness is quickly replaced by the cool touch of something hard. Glancing down, I see the hilt of the knife placed at my back entrance.

I shake my head, whimpering incoherently. My energy wanes as I relentlessly twist under the rope, careful not to expose the progress of my left wrist. Jason forces me back to the center of the table with a single hand, his face mere inches from my own.

"Pity, really. Do you know how hard it is to feign being scared when you've conditioned your brain to feel *nothing*? Lucky for me, you wear your heart on your sleeve. It wasn't hard to mimic everything you felt."

Jason closes the distance between us with his tongue. It glides over my bottom lip before he crashes into me. The kiss is violent and sloppy. Teeth clashing, his tongue explores my own without permission. I break the kiss for enough time to breathe.

"You talk too much," I say breathlessly before I bring his tongue between my teeth and bite down. He growls and shoves me back onto the table. Bringing a hand up, he wipes his bottom lip with his thumb. Jason examines it, dripping red in the light. A grin spreads over his face. The devil reincarnate.

I spit at him, removing any traces of his blood from my mouth. The metallic tinge still lingers.

"It's too bad you didn't confess your love for me sooner, little bat. We could've had so much fun together." He clicks his tongue. "Oh, well. I'll have my fun killing you. Hearing your pretty, little screams as I cut into your soft meat like a well-aged steak."

Jason pulls the knife from my ass and strikes at my hip bone, digging deeper than before. I cry into the night, begging the universe to send someone to hear me. He closes his eyes and inhales in a deep breath before sighing. "Delicious."

From behind, Jason's body is silhouetted by a blinding, white light. I squint my eyes at an attempt to look through the window. Jason mumbles something under his breath before stomping over to the window, his knife graciously forgotten at my side. Seeing my chance, I shift my left wrist free of the rope. Quickly, I take the knife to cut the rest of my binds. I slink off the table, careful to not pad too hard onto the ground. Jason is still staring out the window as I readjust my footing.

Keeping my eyes glued to his back, I take a cautious step towards him. By the grace of some almighty being, he hasn't moved. Readjusting the knife in my grip, I continue my stalk towards him. My breathing is shallow as I try to control the adrenaline coursing through my body.

I'm two steps away from him when he shouts. "You think the cops can save you?"

He turns around to face me. The tip of the blade sinks fast and deep into the side of his abdomen. I use the momentum to shove him back against the wall. The soft, damp fabric of his shirt is gentle against my skin. I push further with the knife until I feel the hardness of the drywall behind him.

Jason looks at me with a mixture of shock and pure evil. He grabs my shoulders, shoving me backwards. I stumble over my footing, falling to the ground with the knife. The wooden floor is unforgiving in my landing. Before I have a chance to shake off the sting, Jason lunges forward. My back flattens against the ground as his body lands on top of me. His attack is cut short as I shove the knife between us. This time, the sharp tip makes contact with his center mass.

Jason stays suspended in the air. The blade puncturing his intestines is the only thing keeping us apart. I shove it deeper, causing the wound to open further as blood gushes from the opening. A guttural cry escapes him as I twist the blade deeper through the soft tissue leaking from orifice. Leaning forward, my lips brush gently against his. A feather light kiss sealing his fate.

"Final girls don't need saving. We save our damned selves," I hiss. I jerk the knife up in a jagged motion. Jason sputters, blooding spraying from his mouth, misting me in the process. He falls off of me as his hands scramble to remove the instrument of death. Crimson liquid oozes in all directions. He reaches out for me, but his hands don't find a hold as his blood-soaked hands slip effortlessly off my naked body. I release the handle and scramble back from his grasp. Coughing overcomes his breathing as he chokes on his own blood, his body sagging. Jason reaches for me again as I stand on weak legs, heading towards the open front door.

The gentle wind coming from the entrance is crisp against my sensitive skin, brushing over each open wound Jason made. Breathing in the chilled night air, I mentally release the demon from deep within. A carnal smile caresses my lips. The lava seeping through my veins soothing every aching part of me, turning numb. The tears stop coming. My breathing evens itself out. My feet ground solid into the earth. I look back to the crumpled body on the floor.

"It's time to die, Jason. Rest in hell."

I turn and walk out into my blinding salvation.

EPILOGUE

ASHE

I shake the cramp out of my hand as I assess the line in front of me. No matter how much I try to prepare for book signings, my hand always gets cranky halfway in. The throng of people snakes all the way back to the bookstore's entrance.

It's release day for my newest novel. This has been the most successful launch since I wrote about our town's gruesome history. I have since transitioned from self published to signing with a publishing house and an agent. My bonus was almost double the market average with the condition that I produce a new novel once a year after the ink dried. Receiving such a huge bonus from a traditional publishing agency is unheard of for my genre. It still amazes me that so many people, seemingly normal people, share in the same morbid fascination in storytelling as I do.

I take a steadying breath and smile at the reader in front of me.

"Good morning," I say, mustering as much politeness as I can.

A petite girl with emerald eyes stares back at me. Her smile is sweet, matching her whimsical outfit. Dark auburn curls frame her bronzed face. She reminds me of a fairy living deep in a wooden cottage. Living off the land. Making her own remedies for what ales her. Frolicking in the open fields under the star light. It tugs at something deep inside me.

I throw up a mental wall between that woeful memory and the present task at hand. I don't have the time or space to think about that now. No one wants to see an author have a mental breakdown on something that should be the happiest day of their life. It'll have to wait for later.

It's been a year since the police saved me from my own nightmare. I was on the brink of hysterics, covered in blood and gore when they found me. Slumped over onto the dampened ground in front of the James' family cabin. According to one of the responding officers, I was mumbling incoherently. My eyes were wild and my reaction to them was violent. It took three of them to drag me from my place on the ground to the warm interior of the ambulance when it arrived.

I spent two days in the ICU and one week in inpatient therapy before they deemed me sane enough to be released. The next month I spent my weekdays in their outpatient program with hours upon hours of therapy, learning coping mechanisms, and writing. The officers assigned to my case didn't dare question me on what happened the night they found me until I was fully cleared. Doctor's orders. They said after what they can only imagine that I went through, my mind and body needed the break. Something about reliving old memories could cause a relapse. Jokes on them, though. Some of the things I witnessed that night I will never be able to remove from my memory. They're scarred into my psyche. My own personal ghosts, forever haunting me day and night. The only way to get a moment's peace was through writing, and from that writing, came this book. This book helped me get back to my new life. So many truths and secrets hidden within these pages, disguised as macabre curiosities.

Rumors spread that my book shared too many similarities to the horrendous events I endured last fall. Luckily for me, the police dismissed me as a person of interest almost immediately. They were vague on what they found at the scene. A detective with kind eyes and a chiseled jawline informed me they found all the evidence they needed to conclude the rampage was completed by The Senior Slayer and his accomplices. I never told them that one of those accomplices was my friend. My lover.

I internally cringe at myself.

Lover.

What a ridiculous term. We didn't even get the chance to love. We fucked. The lust burning our souls into an inferno of passion from the pent up years of attraction. All of that energy only for years of trust to be ripped away with the quick slice of betrayal. Everything I knew was reduced into ash at my feet.

"Oh em GEE!" the girl in front of me squeals, pulling me from my spiraling thoughts.

"I've been waiting so long to meet you. I love all of your work! Ugh. It just speaks to me."

I take her book from her hands and fake a smile back at her.

"Aw, thank you, dear. I know my books aren't *traditional*, but I hope you love this new one as much as I do."

She nods enthusiastically at me, tippy tapping on her feet and silently clapping her hands together.

"I plan on binging it the minute I get home!" she gushes.

My lip thin into a shy smile at her enthusiasm, heat in my cheeks blazing ever so slightly. It never ceases to amaze me how words can connect people in this way.

I ask her for her name and sign her book before wishing her a quiet goodbye. The darkness inside of me shoves at the mental barrier. Looking over to my personal assistant, Myra, I signal with my fingers that I need a break. She rushes over, all rainbows and sunshine with her multicolored dress and wild hair. Such a stark difference from the books she promotes.

Clapping her hands, her singsong voice booms over the audience. "Okay, lovelies. We need to take a short break. You can remain where you're at or get some fresh air. Ms. Nikko will be back to greet all of you in five minutes."

I squeeze Myra's shoulder as I stand and slink towards the bathroom.

I count my blessings when I see both stalls are empty upon entering. Locking the door behind me, I spend my time splashing water on my face to obscure the tears streaming down my cheeks and counting to ten. My breathing is ragged and uneven, gasps of air between silent sobs, as I try to calm my nerves. I repeat my new mantra in my head, credited to the outpatient therapy I completed.

"You are worthy. You are strong. You are not your past."

I lean my body from side to side. Roll my neck slowly back and forth and shake my hands to get the imaginary blood off my skin. After a little shimmy, I square my shoulders. I know I can never rid myself from these little moments of grief, but they get easier each time.

Returning to the sales floor, I note that most of the line has wandered off. Some people are chatting among themselves. Others have wandered outside to enjoy the warm sun against their skin. A few mingle near the cafe waiting on their order.

I take the time to straighten my table. Myra helps me replenish the stack of books behind me for readers who didn't preorder. I check all my pens and chuck the ones that are dead. A smile tugs at my lips when I take in my beautiful tablescape. Myra is always the creative genius with these set ups.

"Do you need anything? I was going to grab a new cup o' Joe and a little snackerdoodle," she asks.

I shake my head. "No, thanks. We're almost done here. I have dinner plans at the tiki lounge."

Myra's eyes widen. A smirk threatens to encompass her composed features.

"Oh, dinner? Or a *dinner* dinner?" She raises her brows at me.

"Fucking hell, Myra. Dinner!" I laugh. "I'm meeting Summer. She just got back from visiting family down south."

Myra's eyes look me up and down. Her lips threaten a smirk behind her professional mask. That wild gleam dances in her eyes.

"Mhm. Whatever, or whoever, helps you sleep at night, honeybuns," she drawls, patting my back before heading towards the cafe.

I roll my eyes, shaking my head as I watch her leave. Incorrigible bitch.

I know it's not professional to become friends with your assistant, but Myra always knows how to keep me on my toes.

A thud erupts from the table in front of me. I startle, staring down at the stack of books in front of me. It's the last three novels I've written. The covers are beat to shit, some of the corners frayed. An oddly colored stain mares the one on top. Gingerly, I use my index finger to push the books flat on the table. It's not unusual for readers to bring past copies to be signed, but never in this condition.

I reach for my pen while I continue inspecting each book.

"Ever the horror lover, are we?" I quip. Grabbing the middle book, I open the cover to the first blank page. "Who am I signing this for?"

A deep timber of a laugh rumbles from the person in front of me. The sound of it makes me pause, triggering some feral piece deep inside. My fingers grip the pen tighter, nearly snapping in half. My mouth is suddenly bone dry. The beat of my heart drowning out the hassle of the book store around me. I lift my eyes slowly.

A tall figure stands before me. Lean muscles shadowed by a bulky sweatshirt. Glassy, black hair leaks from the corners of the hood. The stranger leans onto the table. Strong, pale hands grip the edge. Tattoos peek out from the bottom of their sleeves. The aroma of something eerily familiar engulfs the space between us.

Pineapple and spice and everything not nice...

The hooded head lifts to meet my stare. Dark, golden eyes meet my own.

Blood freezes within my veins. Breath catching in my throat. I can't tear my eyes away.

With a deep inhale, the demon from my nightmares replies, "For the one who got away. For the one who defies all odds. The final girl, forever and always. My little bat."

The End...For Now.

TEASER FROM THE KILLING SECRET

BOOK 2 IN THE FINAL GIRLS NEVER DIE DUET

The following is a chapter from Book 2 in the Final Girls Never Die Duet—The Killing Secret. Please keep in mind this book is a work in progress and the text may differ from the final product.

If you're ready to return to The Killing Game and learn more about Ashe, Jason, and The Senior Slayer, keep reading for an exclusive look into Jason's POV.

And remember—the game's not over until everyone dies.

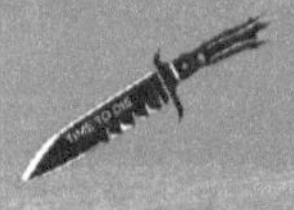

JASON

Throngs of people are bustling outside of the bookstore entrance, stupid book nerds eagerly awaiting for their turn to go inside. Their arms are full of various books, bags, and drinks. A banner hanging in the front window showcases the store's author who's attending today's signing event. Glittery bats and a familiar smile shine back at me in the midday sun. Thank fuck it's October, otherwise this trip would be unbearably hot and sweaty in the worst way.

I stand a few feet away, using a nearby light pole to lean against. This is how you act natural, right? Some sexed up guy in all black sweats smoking a cigarette nonchalantly. *That would never draw any attention.* Well, any unwanted attention. I'm okay if any of these little sluts want to take a ride on the ol' disco stick. It'd be a nice distraction from the real reason why I'm here.

Honestly, I thought I would be better at this. It's not the first time I've approached someone I've been stalking, but this feels different. Fuck me, it is different because this isn't just someone Master sent me to dispatch on his behalf. This is the one that got away. The one who is full of so many secrets, who was full with my rock hard cock, that I didn't know was hiding under the surface. The one I almost killed because I let The Senior Slayer into my head, filling it with putrid lies of deceit, marring my soul with the darkest shadows.

He went so far to threaten the safety of my parents and my baby sister, saying I wouldn't know heartbreak until everything I cared for most dies in front of my very eyes, with no hope in saving them. Luckily, I was able to grovel— yes, grovel; don't even get me started—for their safety. That still leaves me with the predicament of my current fixation. My anxiety has peaked and I can't settle the rock forming in the pit of my stomach.

It's been over a year since I've seen Ashe. A little over four hundred and twenty-five days from that fateful night that changed our lives forever, but who's counting? History was rewritten in blood and sealed in the gruesome death of everyone she loved most. Nothing went as planned that night. No amount of research and stalking prepared Tyler and I for what happened. And that fucker went off script, leaving me scrambling to catch up and play the victim alongside all of them.

And now here I am, against Master's wishes, to check on her. It goes against all the rules he's set for me. I know he's probably here somewhere, watching to make sure I don't fuck this up further. He said, and I quote, "*I have plans for that little cunt. I'll allow you one day. If you fuck this up, it's your balls I'm castrating and eating for dinner tonight.*" Message well received. I much prefer my balls firmly attached below my dick or in the mouth of my favorite goth girl.

So here I am, at this stupid store, waiting for this stupid event to make my move.

Nothing too extravagant. Totally chill compared to my usual antics. Not even a monster dildo in sight to glue to her car. She won't expect to see me. I made sure to feed the papers snippets of information about my alleged stay at the mental hospital and my untimely release. Just enough information so Ashe never forgets about me, about us. I want her memory of me burned into the very essence of her being.

I spent too many years pining at a distance and right when I had the opportunity to make her mine, everything went to shit. Whether she likes it or not, she's mine and I'm never letting her go. 'Til death do us part, regardless if it's my death or hers.

I watch as a gaggle of giggling girls enter through the main entrance, each one a carbon copy of the other, donning athletic shoes, green on green athleisure sets, and ponytails snatched higher than giraffe pussy. The only difference between the group is their jewelry, each wearing whatever color compliments their skin tone the best.

And, yes, I know how to match fucking jewelry to skin tones. Don't insult me like I'm anything close to those cavemen who try to woo women through their big egos and sexist jokes.

It's not the type of reader I'd expect to indulge in Ashe's works, but I guess horror has no archetype. Anyone can connect with the characters Ashe creates and I think that's why people love her so much. She imbues so much authenticity into those characters that people feel drawn to them in lieu of the gore that surrounds them.

It's what drew me to her many years ago. No, it wasn't the bold fashion choices. It wasn't her emotional strength or vast curiosity for the truth. And, while her occasional quips may make me more hardened than diamond, it was her undying loyalty and fierce protection of who she cared most that had me mesmerized. I don't think the universe ever gave me a chance when it came to her. That's why I'm here now because I can never stay away. No matter how hard I try.

Checking my watch, I note the time. My ticket was stamped for a 1 o'clock signing and it's just past 1:05 p.m.

It's showtime, baby!

I collect the stack of books I brought with me. Some of them with yellowed edges and water marks from being stored improperly. I love my books the same way I love my women—well loved and worn out.

Kicking off the light pole, I slowly make my way to the entrance. Holding the door open, I give the approaching women my most dazzling smile. "After you, ladies."

They blush and whisper to each other as they duck beneath my arm to walk inside.

Yup, still got it.

I follow closely behind, keeping enough space between myself and others so as to not raise suspicion. It's a fine line between smoldering stranger and creepy offender. One of my goals is to *not* get arrested today.

I'm confident this little stunt I have planned will be the push she needs to finally leave town. She can't hide in Graveslake forever, using her writing as an excuse to stay home for days at a time. I mean, come on, it was just a few deaths. A little bit of blood and exposed entrails here and there. Nothing out of the ordinary for my little bat, nothing she couldn't have handled. I want her, well no, I *need* her to move to the city. There's too many prying eyes here, who have intimate knowledge of the past, for us to play our game. I want to start fresh in an area that's unmarked from The Senior Slayer's influence.

Standing in line, I let my mind wander, allowing fantasies to smooth over the anxiety bubbling in my stomach. I imagine how thrilling it will be to see the surprise on Ashe's face when she recognizes who I am.

My dick hardens at the thought of seeing her face flushed with shock. The way her eyes dilate when she's speechless and her lips part just enough I can see the moist, fleshy bit of tongue before she swipes it over her bottom lip.

Fuck, I need that tongue on and around my junk.

I redjust my baggy sweatshirt, hoping no one notices I'm actually trying to adjust the half chub in my pants. There's not much to hide any damning evidence that might show I'm more excited than the average person.

Maybe wearing a full sweat suit was a bad idea.

Maybe I could convince a certain someone to take it off of me.

Focus, man. Focus.

Staring ahead, I can see a sliver of blue. Ashe's signature blue hair is vibrant against the beige interior of the bookshop. A poisonous flower blooming in a bland, postmodern jungle. She's seated at a table with books piled high on either side. The center is cleared with colorful pens and markers at her disposal. She's smiling at a reader who's currently gushing over her most recent release, but I can tell her returning sentiment is forced. The way her eyes crinkle in the corner when she's trying to hide how she truly feels is a dead giveaway. Ashe probably thinks she does so well concealing her true feelings, but I've always been able to see past the mask she constantly wears.

The petite reader squeals, jumping for joy over something Ashe just told her, her chocolate brown curls bouncing with each hop. In a hast, she grabs her signed book and shoves it into her bag that's covered in printed marijuana leaves. She waves at Ashe before turning to leave. I take a step closer to the table as the crowd of people shifts forward to allow the next reader to introduce themselves.

Throwing my hood up, I scan the crowd to pass the time when the brunette reaches me, looking up at me as she passes. Green eyes locking with mine. A familiar pang pulls at the stone in my chest where my heart should be. Her heart-shaped face drags up memories filled with light, love, and happiness removed too early from this world.

Her perfume assaults my nose with the warm notes of earth and flowers. A scent that would smell like a warm embrace to others, but for me, it shatters what little humanity I have remaining. I feel possessed by her presence. My body doesn't feel like my own as I track her to the exit of the book store. She turns as she reaches for the door and blows me a kiss.

The heart that I didn't know still existed shatters into a million pieces.

Tears prick behind my eyes.

I shutter, attempting to drag in a breath of air, as I try to compose myself.

A death rattle of my long, lost friend drowns out the thud of my erratic heartbeat. It's chilled claws digging its way through my body.

"Sam," I hear myself whisper.

My body is becoming numb, a dissociative episode lingering on the fringes of my already frayed nerves. The store around me blurs into a cave of sorrow. It's taken every ounce of strength I had this year to keep myself stitched together, to get to this point, and my mental fortitude was just destroyed by the remembrance of my former life.

Time feels like it's standing still and yet moving at light speed around me.

It isn't until the older lady standing behind me shoves into my shoulder with surprising force.

"Boy, either move forward or get out of line."

My body feels sluggish as I turn to look at her. A stout woman who looks as mean as she sounds. And just as quickly as I was longing for my dead friend, I'm back to envisioning the best way to gut this cow like the rude bitch she is.

Opting to not make a scene and blow my cover, I give the mild version of what I wish I could say to her.

"It's a line. You're waiting whether I move two feet forward or not. Relax, Grandmother Cunt."

In an act of dramatics anyone could have guessed, the

woman huffs in disgust before mumbling she's going to get the manager as she leaves the line.

I roll my eyes. Turning back to the line, there's an absence of blue in front of me.

Fucking hell.

I swear to everything unholy, if I missed my one chance to speak with my girl because this twat distracted me, I'm going to lose it.

Her assistant projects over the crowd to announce her departure. "Alright, my loves. We're going to take a break. Miss Nikko will be back in five minutes."

I frantically scan the area behind the table to locate Ashe. Most of the crowd has dispersed to other areas of the floor, many finding their home in line at the adjacent coffee shop. Continuing my search, I find her in the back of the store slipping into the women's bathroom, her face taking on a ghostly hue that rivals my own pallid complexion. The tremble of her bottom lip tells me everything I need to know.

She's not taking a bathroom break. She's about to have a full blown panic attack, probably for the same reason I almost went into catatonia.

Even a year after the slayings and the heaps of therapy, Ashe can't face the smallest remembrance of her dearly departed friend.

And it's at that moment that I decide maybe now wouldn't be the best time to ambush her in the bathroom to make my big come back. While I'm totally down for some kinky fuckery in the bathroom, that deviates from the plan.

I make my way to the closest spiral rack and pretend to flip through the various novellas on display. Keeping one eye on the bathroom and the table, I eagerly await for her return to ensure I'm the first one in line.

After what feels like an eternity of browsing, I check my phone. Right on cue, Ashe emerges from the bathroom at the five minute mark. Her face is more vibrant and that same fake smile is slipped into place.

She speaks with her assistant as she returns to her table. Their voices are muffled, getting lost in the drone of chatter throughout the space. Something said between them makes her audibly laugh, the sound making my cock twitch to life again.

With a renewed sense of urgency, I side step my way around a few readers into the front of the line. No one says anything. No one ever does...well, expect the old hag from earlier, who I've noticed is nowhere to be seen now.

I shift the bag of books and retrieve the stack, keeping the spines evenly placed together. The top and bottom books are in pristine condition since I only bought them a few days ago. The middle, however, I've had since it was released during her first publication. The first horror book Ashe ever released into the big, bad world.

She was so nervous during that first release she didn't sleep for two days once it went live. I remember Colton and I going to her place, forcing her to shut down her laptop and phone in order to have some time to tend to her basic needs. You can't live off of anxiety and caffeine forever.

The middle book is my most prized possession, though it doesn't look like it. It's definitely taken a beating, maybe had a drink or two spilled on it. A blood stain here or there. But I refuse to buy a new one. I'm keeping this bad boy until it falls apart.

I'm giddy as I stand at the front of the line, waiting to be ushered forward by her assistant. I think I caught her name

—Myra. And then something about someone named Summer. I run through the mental list of names associated with my little bat and the name doesn't sound familiar. I'll need to do research later tonight to get a better understanding of *who* that is and why they're important.

I swear to god if Ashe found herself a new play thing before I had my chance with her, I'll fucking lose it.

Assistant Myra waves me forward with a sickly sweet smile before skittering away to fuss over the boxes of books in the background.

Keeping my head low to allow the hood to disguise my face, I drop the pile of books onto the table.

Ashe jumps in her seat, but she recovers quickly. My lips pull upward as excitement renews within me.

At least her little freak out didn't completely numb her senses.

That's good, really good.

Darkness begins to creep its way back into my consciousness. Tendrils of shadows blanketing over my sanity. It takes every bit of willpower to not hop in place like a giddy child waiting to surprise their parents with a new art project.

Ashe straightens in her seat, taking a breath. Reaching forward, her brows furrow as she inspects the books laying on the table. Her hands delicately push the books apart so they're all evenly placed. She picks each one up, inspecting their covers and then lays them down in a line again.

"Ever the horror lover, are we?" Ashe grabs the pen closest to her and picks the middle book from the pile. My eyes track her movements. Her hands glide over the cover to find the title page to sign her name. "Who am I signing this for?"

Her voice whispers to the darkness inside me, smooth

as silk and sweet as honey. My soul begs to reach out and take her as my own.

Fuck, fuck, fuck.

Keep it together, Vega.

But the darkness is winning. I'm losing my mind just being here in front of her.

A rumble of laughter rolls out of me, either from anxiety or sheer psychosis.

I reach down to grip the table, allowing the darkness to flow freely. I keep my head low, my face still shielded with my hair and the hood. I can feel the fleece fabric of my sweatshirt straining over my muscles as my arms flex. The movement causes the sleeves to roll slightly, allowing ample view of my tattoos.

I watch, transfixed, until I see the moment reality clicks into place for Ashe.

Her nostrils flare at the realization. Eyes dilate on command in my presence as I anticipated.

I lift my head to lock my gaze to her steely blue, fear and lust swirling in a magnificent trial of will behind those eyes. We exist together, in this space, for what feels like an eternity. So many silent words pass between us, but none are the words I finally say when I open my mouth to break the silence.

"For the one who got away. For the one who defies all odds. The final girl, forever and always. My little bat."

Her chair skitters back as she bolts up. Ashe doesn't say a word as she grabs her small, leather backpack in a panic and runs out of the store, tripping over a book display on her way out. She doesn't look back as she leaves.

"Ashe?" her assistant calls. "Honey, where the hell are you going?"

I watch as she rushes out the front door and disappears

into the parking lot. When I turn around, her assistant is glaring at me. I just shrug, flashing a panty dropping smirk. "I have that effect on women. What can I say?"

Her assistant huffs before rushing off to speak with a manager standing by the checkout counter, who looks just as confused from the abrupt ending of the signing event.

I collect my books and readjust the hood atop my head. Swiping a stray piece of hair off my forehead, I stride towards the exit. I take note of all the eyes on me as I leave the bookstore, pride swelling inside at the realization this was a job well done, if even the strangers know something about my presence was wrong.

And just like that, a little bat fell directly into my trap.

TIME TO DIE

AUTHOR'S NOTES

If you've made it this far, congratulations! You survived the killing game...for now.

I am forever grateful you took a chance on my story. I hope Ashe inspires you in the same way she inspires me. While horror can be gory and entertaining, it also opens the door for a deeper conversation.

My goal through these stories are to explore what it truly means to be the final girl. What strength and courage is needed in order to make it to the end? How does that affect the character's mental health? There's so much more to a final girl that Hollywood frequently chooses to forget (or intentionally ignore). I'm not an expert, but I think this kind of representation is validating. Despite everything, Ashe is resilient. She encompasses so many traits I wish I had when I was going through my own nightmares.

As for the Senior Slayer and Jason, only time will tell if their story will be told. I never would have thought Jason was going to make it to the epilogue. My original plot had everyone dying in the end. He had other plans and decided his story wasn't finished. Go figure, Jason takes after his namesake, becoming the haunting, god-like killer all the best slasher movies embody. I'm still annoyed he hijacked my ending, but I also think it's better for it.

If there's one thing you take away from this book, please let it be this: YOUR MENTAL HEALTH MATTERS. No matter what you go through, you belong here with us. And if you need to shout into the void or ask for help, please use the resources below.

National Crisis Hotline: 800-273-8255

Text: 988

TIME TO DIE

ACKNOWLEDGMENTS

First: a long, warm, tear-filled (not really tears, maybe a sheepish smile and a middle finger, but just imagine it) thank you to my amazing partner. I wouldn't be here writing this page if not for you. You gave me the courage and safety to pursue my dreams. My cheerleader, brainstorming partner, scene coordinator, weapons expert, and alpha reader. Kalin, I love you more than the moon and the stars. <3

Second: thank you to the rest of my alpha readers - Char, Maddie, Donovan, Katie, Hayley, Jay, Fran, Kalah, and Ashley. To all my friends, both on Booksta and Drinkin' Bros, THANK YOU for believing in me. Thank you for putting up with my inconsistent uploading of new chapters and redundant use of "the blood pounded in my ears". There were so many times I questioned if I truly wanted to do this and y'all were always there to push me forward. Your words of encouragement and your excitement over these characters does not go unnoticed. I'm forever grateful to have you along for this journey.

Another thank you to all my amazing contributors to make this book happen:

Hannah, thank you for sliding into my DM's and being so enthusiastic about my manuscript, even as a first timer. A baby author. You never doubted my talent. The tender love and care for this story while keeping my voice genuine, along with an endless supply of entertaining side commentary, is BEYOND appreciated. Also, thank you for putting up with my frequent misuse of commas. (I swear, they're like sprinkles. They belong everywhere.)

Shay, Valkyrie, my little goth gremlin. I'm convinced fate brought us together. Who would've known that a doomscroll for cover art would lead to such an amazing relationship. I admire your honesty with deadlines and your attention to detail. I appreciate that you allow me to change my mind over and over and over again. I've watched your talent soar since we met and I can't wait to see where the book world takes you. I'm so deeply honored to have you on my team (like, literally, you are stuck with me. I'm basically adopted at this point.) and to work on future books together. I love you, chaos twin.

And, Bria. Sweet, kind, helpful, persistent Bria. I don't have much words to say because I'm word vomiting to you almost daily. However, I never would have thought our interactions would become such a wonderful and powerful connection in my life. To think, at one point in time, I thought you were too _cool_ for little 'ol me! Thank you for the bottom of my heart for sharing your knowledge, your trials and errors, our endless content brainstorming sessions, and you endless love. I hope one day to meet you IRL, so I can give you the biggest hug and we can finally have our wine 'n pizza movie night.

Also, thank you to the online book community. Thank you to all my reader friends for sharing their favorite/least favorite tropes with me. Thank you to all my author friends for your unending support, suggestions for fellow vendors, and shouting my book from the rooftops. This is a community I was missing for so long. I found a piece of myself again through your welcoming kindness.

Lastly— You. The reader. I know I already thanked you, but it bares saying again. Thank you! Thank you for picking this book up. Thank you for reading it, no matter if it was 30 pages or 30 chapters. Thank you for taking a chance on me. I hope you loved this story and I hope you enjoy more in the future.

ONE LAST THING...

If you're totally awesome, and feel inclined, please leave me a review.

My book is active on Goodreads, Storygraph, and Amazon. Reviews help publishers and retailers see how readers spend their money. More reviews means a higher chance for more stories in the future.

Also, mistakes happen! If you find any typos, please contact me directly at: hello@authorsagemitchell.com. Reporting typos to Amazon can blacklist authors from releasing new works.

Feeling social? Follow me!
Instagram- @SagesBookstack
TikTok- @SagesBookstack
Goodreads- Sage Mitchell

ABOUT THE AUTHOR

Sage Mitchell is the sassy altar ego of a Midwestern girl who chooses to remain semi-anonymous. Sage grew up in the northwoods where she obsessed over reading, wrote fantastical poetry and prose in private, loved spooky things, and binged watched Supernatural more than 100 times.

Attending the University of Wisconsin – Whitewater, Sage obtained a Bachelors of Science Education degree specializing in English; along with a minor in Anthropology. She spent the majority of her 20's teaching students that reading is an experience and it's accessible for everyone (No, seriously, even audiobooks and comics). While she loved her work, the gremlin in the back of her mind kept nagging at her to write a book. That nagging quickly turned into a lifelong goal.

Now, Sage lives with her fur baby and husband on the West Coast. Her debut horror novel, The Killing Game, is just the start of her venture into the author world. When she's not cozying up at home with a book, going to Disneyland with her partner, or connecting with her bookish online community, Sage is holed up finding the next great story to write.

https://www.authorsagemitchell.com

www.ingramcontent.com/pod-product-compliance
Lightning Source LLC
Chambersburg PA
CBHW051423130726
47987CB00005B/1889